MISSION 4

HAMMERHEAD

mars
DIARIES

MISSION 4

HAMMERHEAD

SIGMUND BROUWER

TYNDALE
KIDS

TYNDALE HOUSE PUBLISHERS, INC.
WHEATON, ILLINOIS

Visit the exciting Web site for kids at www.cool2read.com
and the Mars Diaries Web site at www.marsdiaries.com

You can contact Sigmund Brouwer through his Web site at
www.coolreading.com

Designed by Justin Ahrens

Edited by Ramona Cramer Tucker

ISBN 0-8423-4307-5, mass paper

Printed in the United States of America

07   06   05   04   03
7   6   5   4   3   2

THIS SERIES IS DEDICATED
IN MEMORY OF MARTYN GODFREY.

Martyn, you wrote books that reached all of us kids at heart. You wrote them because you really cared. We all miss you.

CHAPTER 1

Ambush!

Rawling McTigre, the director of the Mars Project, had warned me that, on this practice run in the Hammerhead space torpedo, I wouldn't be alone in the black emptiness 3,500 miles above the planet. But I'd already circled Phobos, one of the Martian moons, twice and seen nothing, so it was a complete surprise when my heat radar buzzed with movement from below.

Actually, it's wrong to say I had seen nothing.

What I'd really seen was the silver glint of sunlight bouncing off Phobos. To do that, I'd raced at the moon with the sun behind me. At the speed I moved in the Hammerhead, the moon was almost invisible coming from any other angle. It was so tiny, and the backdrop of deep space so totally dark, except for the pinpoints of stars.

Without the sun at my back, straining for visual contact with Phobos was like trying to see a black marble hanging in front of a black velvet curtain.

It was also wrong to say the movement came from below.

In space, there *is* no up and down. It's difficult, though, not to think that way because I'm so used to living in gravity, weak as it is on Mars. So I thought of the Hammerhead's stabilizer fin as the top.

When the movement came from the belly side of the space torpedo, my mind instinctively told me it was below.

Just like my mind instinctively told me to roll the Hammerhead away from the movement.

In one way, rolling my space torpedo was as easy as thinking it should roll. It's similar to how you move your arms or your legs. Your brain wills it to happen, and the wiring of your nervous system sends a message to your muscles. Then chemical reactions take place in your muscles' cells and they burn energy, causing you to move.

It was the same way with the Hammerhead. My mind, connected to the computer, willed it to roll and it obeyed instantly. But it was really the computer on board that did all the hard work. It ignited a series of tiny flares along the stabilizer nozzles, allowing the torpedo to react as though it were flying through the friction of an atmosphere, not the vacuum of outer space.

I rolled hard to my right, then hard left, then downward in a tight circle that brought the giant crescent of Mars into my visual.

The top of the massive red ball shimmered with an eerie whiteness, the thin layer of carbon dioxide that covered the planet. And behind it was the glow of the sun.

But I didn't have time to admire this beauty. The planet was getting closer—fast.

I told myself I wouldn't crash, that its closeness was just an illusion because it filled so much of my horizon. After all, the top of the Martian atmosphere was still over 3,000 miles away.

But I was moving at over four miles per second. That

meant if I didn't change direction within the next 10 minutes, I'd get fried to a crisp upon reentry.

I rolled upward, back toward Phobos, hoping to buy some time.

I didn't even bother trying to get a visual confirmation of my pursuer. Because of Rawling's earlier warning, I didn't need to see what was chasing me to know it was another space torpedo. This was the ultimate test of my pilot skills. Against another pilot.

I knew if I looked, I wouldn't be able to see the other space torpedo anyway. My Hammerhead was hardly longer and wider than a human body. Plus, space torpedos are painted black, so they're almost impossible to detect visually in space from more than a hundred yards away.

Right now, with the other pilot chasing me, I was locked in a whirling dance with another space torpedo a hundred miles away, with both of us ducking and bobbing at around 15,000 miles per hour. Not even the best eyes in the universe would be able to watch this dogfight.

No, the only way I could detect the other space torpedo was with heat radar. Tiny as the vent flares were, the heat they produced showed up on radar like mushrooms as big as thunderstorms. Especially in the absolute cold of outer space.

That was good for me, being able to track the other space torpedo as easily as watching a storm cross the sky. But it also meant the pilot of the other torpedo could follow my movement too.

And my Hammerhead was the lead torpedo, a sitting duck in the computer target sights of the pilot behind me.

I made a quick decision. I flared all of my vents equally for an instant. I knew my direction wouldn't change. But it would cause a big blast of heat, hopefully blinding the pilot behind me.

An instant later, I shut down all my vents, knowing my Hammerhead was now shooting through the mushroom of heat I'd just created.

I exited the other side of the heat mushroom with no power or flares to give away my presence. To the heat radar of the pilot behind me, my Hammerhead was as black and cold as outer space itself. I was now invisible.

I congratulated myself for my smart move.

Then I panicked. There was no heat mushroom on *my* radar either. The pilot behind me must have done the same thing—shut down all vent flares.

It could only mean one thing. The pilot had guessed my move and taken a directional reading of my flight path just before I shut down my vents.

I knew I was dead. Without vent flares to control the direction of my Hammerhead, I wouldn't be able to change direction until I reactivated them. It would take my computer 30 seconds to run through its preignition checklist. In space warfare, 30 seconds was eternity, because torpedo computers reacted much more quickly than human brains.

In 30 seconds, the computer of the torpedo behind me would figure out my line of travel and shoot me with a laser before I could reactivate and change direction.

Only 20 seconds left.

White flashed over my visual from the other torpedo's target scanner. I was dead center in the laser target controls.

I swallowed hard, preparing myself for the red killer-flash that would follow in an instant, blowing my spacecraft to shreds. The explosion of my Hammerhead torpedo would be soundless since you can't hear screams in the vacuum of outer space.

Another white flash hit me instead.

I jumped. The target scanner behind me didn't need confirmation.

A third white flash.

There was still no red laser to superheat the fuel tanks and blow the Hammerhead apart.

I didn't understand. Three times I'd been right in the other pilot's sights. Why hadn't the other pilot fired the laser pulse?

Without warning, my vents reactivated at the 30-second mark. I rolled, safely out of the way.

I looped, scanning my heat radar again to find the other space torpedo.

Then my visual and my consciousness melted into black nothingness.

CHAPTER 2

"I don't get it," I said to Rawling McTigre. "The pilot of the other space torp had me dead and let me go. What kind of computer program is that?"

A minute earlier the blackout of all my thoughts had signaled the end of my flight simulator program. I was brought out of virtual reality and back to my body in a lab room under the Mars Dome.

I was still sweating from the effort, and my arm muscles shook from stress. I really looked forward to a glass of water.

Rawling leaned forward to unstrap me. Whenever I connected to the computer through virtual reality, my body was secured on a bed so I couldn't roll loose and break the connection.

"Could you be wrong, Tyce?" Rawling asked. "I know it's almost inconceivable that you might make a mistake, but . . ."

"Hah, hah," I said. "Very funny."

Rawling scratched his short, dark hair and smiled, the way he always did when he teased me.

I'd known him all my life, long before he'd been promoted from one of the two medical doctors under the Mars Dome to director of the entire Project. Though he was in his mid-40s and I was only 14 (in Earth years), Rawling was my best friend. After all, until a few months ago, I'd been the only kid under the dome. Ever since I could remember, Rawling had worked with me for hours every day, training me in a virtual-reality program. I was learning to control a robot body as if it were my own.

Over the last month, we had gone beyond the robot body. Rawling was supervising me as I learned the controls of a space torpedo we had nicknamed "Hammerhead," because it looked so much like the shark I'd seen on Earth DVD-gigaroms.

"Do you think that's been programmed?" I asked. "For the other pilot to show mercy?"

"That would surprise me. Mercy is something human." Rawling helped me sit up, then handed me a glass of water. He knew I always needed it badly when I exited virtual reality. "You were in a flight simulation program. The other pilot was simply computer generated. It's not like there was another human linked into the program."

"It's also human to guess about my heat-vent trick."

Instead of asking me what I meant, Rawling raised an eyebrow, something I practiced myself when I knew people weren't looking.

"Heat-vent trick," I repeated, still sitting on the bed and facing him. I drank deeply from the water before I continued. "At the beginning of the week, when you told me I only had a few days left to get ready for an enemy pilot, I planned to try the heat-vent trick during this flight simulation."

That wasn't quite true. I hadn't planned this trick all by myself. The only other kid under the dome was Ashley Jordan, a recent Mars arrival who'd become my friend. I'd talked to her about it, and together we'd come up with the idea.

"It's a way to make a light explosion in the enemy pilot's radar," I continued. "Then you coast out of the backside of it with so little power that you can't be tracked by heat radar."

Next I explained to Rawling how I had done it.

"Pretty good," he said, scratching his short, dark hair and nodding enthusiastically. "Except for the 30 seconds you had to wait to reignite the stabilizer vents and get directional power again. I'm very, very surprised that the computer program was able to make an adjustment to let the pilot track you. So let me say this again. Maybe it was a mistake, you thinking you were in the target scanner. I mean, according to this program, the enemy pilot is supposed to destroy you at the first opportunity."

"Sure," I said, not convinced. I'd been flashed three times with the target scanner's white laser beam. Maybe once was my imagination, but not three times. Was it possible the other pilot had given me three chances instead of blowing me away at the first opportunity? If so, the enemy pilot sounded too human to be computer generated. Almost as if the pilot knew me or something.

Rawling helped me from the bed and into my wheelchair.

"I have a couple of questions," I said. With my hands, I rocked the wheels back and forth. It was something I did when I was restless, like other people might tap their fingers.

"Fire away," he said with a grin. Like he knew it was a pun based on the space torpedo program I'd just gone through.

"Why a space torpedo?" I asked. "Don't get me wrong.

After all those years of working with a robot, this Hammerhead is a lot of fun. And you know I love being in outer space, even if it's just virtual reality. Only . . ."

"Only what?"

"It seems a waste."

"Waste?" Rawling repeated.

"I know these virtual-reality computer training programs cost millions and millions of dollars to develop," I said. "So why would the government spend all this money to train anyone to fly something that doesn't exist?"

Rawling walked past me and shut the door. Then he spoke so quietly that I could barely hear him. "I guess now is as good a time as any to tell you. . . . Remember when the last shuttle arrived?"

Of course I did. Shuttles only arrived from Earth every three years. They were the lifeblood of the Mars Project, bringing new scientists and technicians and supplies, then returning to Earth with the scientists and tekkies who had finished their duty. As if that wasn't enough reason for me to remember, my dad was a space pilot, and he'd returned to Mars with the last shuttle. After getting to know him all over again, I'd finally started to like having him around.

"The Hammerhead does exist, Tyce," Rawling said. "And it arrived with that last shuttle."

"What! There really is a Hammerhead?"

This was great. I could go into space. I could fly at speeds that no human ever flew. I could—

"Don't get too excited." He spoke so sharply that I blinked. "Sorry." He sighed. "The responsibilities that come with being director sometimes . . ."

I waited for him to finish. Suddenly the lines in his face seemed much deeper, and I saw a thicker streak of gray in his hair.

"Tyce, if you don't learn to fly the Hammerhead like it's part of your body, there's a good chance the dome won't exist in another few months."

CHAPTER 3

09.15.2039

Computer notes, I guess, are the only diary I, Tyce Sanders, have. It's a habit I started a few months ago when it looked like the dome was running out of oxygen. I've found that writing into my computer is a great way to sort out my thoughts.

And right now, after what Rawling explained to me, I have plenty to sort out.

It's about a comet. A giant killer comet.

Rawling gave me the rundown. Far beyond the solar system, thousands, millions, or maybe even trillions of comets circle our sun in orbits that take them hundreds or thousands of years. They lurk out in the darkness, invisible because they are too far away for the sun to warm them. Every once in a while, the gravity of a nearby star will nudge them out of their orbit, sending them into the outer edges of the solar system. If Jupiter's massive gravity pulls them closer, their orbit swings them toward the sun. That means the comet will then pass the inner planets of Mars and Earth and Venus and Mercury. Sometimes the comet will hit the sun directly, blooming in incredible cosmic fireworks. Most of the time the comet flashes past the sun and heads back out to the darkness of the outer solar system, never to be seen again. But if its orbit has been changed enough, it will return again and again and again, like Halley's comet, which passes by the Earth every 76 years.

Comets are made of three parts. The *heart* is a big chunk of rock and ice. Picture a big black potato, hundreds of feet wide or up to 15 miles across. The *coma* is the sphere of gas and dust that surrounds the rock. And following behind is the *tail*—ice and dust released by the sun's heat. Even though a comet might only be a couple of miles wide, its tail can grow into a stream in the solar wind as long as a hundred million miles, reflecting the light of the sun in a dazzling display. It's the tail of the comet that's so beautiful.

And the heart that's so dangerous.

Look at it this way. Comets travel at 150,000 miles per hour. Even a small chunk of rock—say half the size of a football field—can make a crater a mile wide if it hits a planet. All it would take is the impact of a comet a couple of miles wide to destroy all life on Earth.

The comet Rawling was talking about was 12 miles wide. It—

"Hello, Mr. Sanders. Hello, Mrs. Sanders."
I knew that voice.

"Hello, Ashley," Mom answered. "Tyce is at his computer. Go on in."

Which meant Ashley would be at my door in a few seconds. Our mini-dome, like everyone else's under the main dome, has two office-bedrooms with a common living space in the middle. Mom and Dad weren't able to use their second room as an office, because that had become my bedroom. We didn't need a kitchen, since we never had anything to cook. Instead, a small microwave oven hung on the far wall; it was used to heat nutrient-tubes or "nute-tubes" as I called them—the food we ate on Mars. Another door at the back of the living space led to a tiny bathroom. It wasn't much. From what I've read about Earth homes, our mini-dome had less space in it than the size of two average bedrooms. It didn't take long to cross something that small.

I swung my wheelchair away from the computer and toward the door.

"Hello, Tyce," Ashley said from the doorway with her usual big grin.

Ashley and her father, an expert in artificial-intelligence computers, had arrived in June with the last shuttle from Earth. She was the only person close to my age under the dome. And with her straight, black hair cut short and serious and her almond-shaped eyes, she sometimes looked older than her 13 Earth years—especially when she wasn't smiling.

"Hey," I said. She and I usually went up to the dome telescope after supper. But the telescope had been malfunctioning for the last couple of weeks, and the tekkie in charge hadn't been able to fix it yet. Just as well. The last thing I wanted was to look for a tiny bullet of deadly light that would show the comet getting closer to Mars by 150,000 miles every hour.

"Hey, back," she said. Then she frowned. "What's wrong?"

"Nothing."

"Give me a break," she said. "I can tell when something's bothering you."

She pulled up a chair so that we were facing each other. It hadn't taken Ashley long to get used to the fact that I was in a wheelchair. When she and I first met, I had explained to her what I would explain to anybody.

I was the first person to be born on Mars—much to the previous Mars Project director's shock. No one had expected Kristy Wallace, a scientist and one of the first colonists, and Chase Sanders, a space pilot, to fall in love during the eight-month journey from Earth to Mars. When they married and I was born half a Mars year later (that's almost a full Earth year), it was tough for the colony. They hadn't planned on any marriages or babies until the colony was better established. After all, with ships only arriving every three years, cargo space is very, very expensive. There's no room for baby items—or a motorized wheelchair.

But you don't have to feel sorry for me—even if I am in a wheelchair because of an experimental spine operation gone wrong.

"Well," Ashley said bluntly, "talk to me."

"If an asteroid was going to hit a planet, how would you stop it?"

She laughed. "That is so 20th century, Tyce. I mean, all you need to do is watch some of those ancient premillennium movies where everyone on Earth is doomed because of a giant asteroid."

"And?" I insisted.

"The solution is so simple I can't believe you're asking. Attach a rocket engine to the asteroid and change its orbit. Alter it by a degree or two, and it misses the planet. Or blow it apart with a nuclear weapon. People stopped worrying about asteroids hitting the Earth long before we were born."

Seeing my face, she stopped laughing. "Tyce, you still look worried."

Rawling was going to make the announcement the next morning, and I'd already told Mom and Dad at supper, so it was all right to discuss it with Ashley. She knew I worked with the robot and would find it interesting that now I was learning to fly a space torpedo.

"And what if the asteroid broke up into hundreds of smaller pieces before you could divert it?" I asked. "What if any of those pieces was big enough to destroy this entire dome? And what if all of those hundreds of pieces were only two months away from hitting us?"

"Then," she said with total seriousness, "I would start to pray. Very hard."

"You can start tonight," I said.

She inhaled sharply.

Then I told her what Rawling had explained to me.

Back in the last century, in 1994, a comet named Shoemaker-Levy 9 appeared from out of the darkness beyond the solar system, like some sort of prehistoric shark cruising up from the unexplored depths of the ocean. Jupiter's massive gravity pulled Shoemaker-Levy 9 closer and closer, and the comet crumpled. Splitting into 20 pieces, it slammed into Jupiter's upper atmosphere. Each explosion released the energy of a gigantic nuclear bomb, and it took over a year for the black clouds of the explosion to disappear from the telescopes aimed at Jupiter from Earth.

Now another comet was headed our way, like a lone black rocket of death. From what we were told by the Earth scientists, they expected this one, too, to break up as it passed Jupiter. The pieces, however, would miss Jupiter completely this time—and intercept Mars a few months later.

Unlike Jupiter, Mars has no atmosphere thousands of miles high to absorb the chunks of comet. Compared to Jupiter, Mars is the size of a marble. If only a few of those pieces hit anywhere on the planet, the impact would destroy the dome. If all those pieces hit, it could shatter the planet completely, sending a shock wave into the inner solar system. And with chunks of Mars flying in all directions, there was a big, big possibility that the Earth would be hit several months later by debris.

Rawling said it was my job to stop the comet before it stopped us.

CHAPTER 4

"Today's a workday," Rawling said. "Try to make it as short as possible. We want you in the virtual Hammerhead for at least a couple of hours."

I was back in the lab again. Earlier than usual. Considering how important it was for me to fly a Hammerhead in space, Mom and Dad and Rawling had agreed that my schoolwork could be put aside for now.

"Work?" I said. "I was hoping to see the actual Hammerhead. You know, for inspiration."

"Work," Rawling said firmly. "We want you to try something on the dome telescope. Blowing sand out of some rotational gears. I'm hoping that's the problem. We need the telescope operational to allow us to track the pieces of comet as it gets closer. Right now we're going blindly on the advice of Earth scientists who have to watch it from 50 million miles further away. We can't afford to make any errors as we track the pieces of comet. Last time we did that kind of maintenance we had to send tekkies up in space suits. Not only did it take them hours, it was dangerous work up there. You, on the other hand . . ."

He didn't really mean me. He meant the robot that I controlled because of the operation that had crippled me when I was a kid. I'd written all about it in my journal earlier:

> In virtual reality, you put on a surround-sight helmet that gives you a three-dimensional view of a scene on a computer program. The helmet is wired so that when you turn your head, it directs the computer program to shift the scene as if you were there in real life. Sounds generated by the program reach your ears, making the scene seem even more real. Because you're wearing a wired jacket and gloves, the arms and hands you see in your surround-sight picture move wherever you move your own arms and hands.
>
> But here's what you might not have thought about when it comes to virtual reality: when you take off the surround-sight helmet and the jacket and gloves that are wired to a computer, you're actually still in a virtual-reality suit. Your body.
>
> Rawling was the one who explained it best to me.
>
> You see, your brain doesn't see anything. It doesn't hear anything. It doesn't smell anything. It doesn't taste anything. It doesn't feel anything. Instead, it takes all the information that's delivered to it by your nerve endings from your eyes, ears, nose, tongue, skin, or bones, and translates that information.
>
> In other words, the body is like an amazing 24-hour-a-day virtual-reality suit that can power itself by eating food and heal itself when parts get cut or broken. It moves on two legs, has two arms to pick things up, and is equipped to give information

through all five senses. Except instead of taking you through virtual reality, a made-up world, your body takes you through the real world.

What if your brain could be wired directly into a robot? Then wouldn't you be able to see, hear, and do everything the robot could?

Well, that's me. The first human to be able to control a robot as if it were an extension of the brain. It began with that operation when I was little and too young to remember. A special rod, hardly thicker than a needle, had been inserted directly into my spinal column, just above the top of my shoulder blades. From that rod, thousands of tiny biological implants—they look like hairs—stick out of the end of the needle into the middle of my spinal column. Each fiber transmits tiny impulses of electricity, allowing my brain to control a robot's computer.

This was all part of the long-term plan to develop Mars: to use robots to explore the planet. Humans need oxygen and water and heat to survive on the surface. Robots don't. But robots can't think like humans. From all my years of train-ing in a computer simulation program, my mind knew all the muscle moves it takes to handle the virtual-reality controls. Handling the robot is no different, except instead of actually moving my muscles, I imagine I'm moving the muscles. My brain then sends the proper nerve impulses to the robot, and it moves the way I made the robot move in the virtual-reality computer program.

I admit, it is cool. Almost worth being in a wheelchair.

"Rawling, I thought the purpose of all this was to be able to explore the universe. You know, go boldly with a robot where no man has gone before."

"That too," he said. "Just not now. If you want to feel good about this kind of work, think of what the robot body cost the space program. That makes your boring maintenance work worth millions of dollars per hour."

Rawling helped me out of my wheelchair and onto the narrow medical bed. Then he began to strap me in place. What had been exciting a few months earlier was now routine.

I wore a snug military-blue jumpsuit, like everyone else under the dome. There was a difference, however. An antenna was sewn into this jumpsuit. It connected with the plug at the bottom of my neck. Across the room was a receiver that transmitted signals between the bodysuit antenna and the computer drive of the robot. It worked just like the remote control of a television set, with two differences. Television remotes used infrared and were limited in distance. This receiver used X-ray waves and had a 100-mile range.

"For all those millions per hour, you want me to climb the ladder outside the dome?" I asked Rawling.

"Right. Tekkies have already set up the robot with a backpack and compressed air tank. All you have to do is blow sand out of the exposed gears. Shouldn't take much more than five minutes. Then you can get back to the Hammerhead virtual-reality program. The sooner you've got the training in, the sooner we can get you into space."

That was a good incentive. A very good incentive.

I nodded. "Checklist."

"Checklist," Rawling replied.

He made me go through it every time. He said it was like

flying an airplane on Earth. There was no room for mistakes.

"First," I said, "no robot contact with any electrical sources."

"Check."

After all, my spinal nerves were attached to the plug. Any electrical current going into or through the robot could do serious damage to the robot—and to my own brain.

Rawling snugged down the straps across my stomach and chest to keep me from moving and disengaging the plug.

"Second," I said, continuing the list, "I disengage instantly at the first warning of any damage to the robot's computer drive."

All I needed to do to disengage was mentally shout the word *Stop!*

"Check," he answered.

Rawling placed a blindfold over my eyes and strapped my head in position. While I controlled the robot body, it was important for me not to be distracted.

"The robot is at the dome entrance?" I asked.

"Outside the dome entrance. The tekkies moved it there already to save you the time of clearing the double entrance. And when you're finished, leave it out there too. The tekkies will move it back in. That should save you 10 minutes in each direction. That will give you an extra 20 minutes on the Hammerhead program."

"Robot battery at full power?"

"Yes."

"Unplugged from all sources of electrical power?"

I already knew the answer. So did Rawling. If the robot was outside the dome, it was definitely unplugged. But

Rawling was very strict about going through the entire checklist.

"Unplugged," he answered.

"I guess we're ready then," I said. "If I have any other questions, I'll radio them in to you from the top of the dome."

"Checklist complete," Rawling said. He placed ear protectors on as the last step. I was soundproofed and ready to go.

I waited.

By now the sensation was familiar. In the darkness and silence of entering the robot computer, it felt like I was falling off a high, invisible cliff into a deep, invisible hole.

I kept falling and falling and falling. . . .

CHAPTER 5

When my imaginary fall ended, I was on the surface of the planet Mars.

Although my body was still strapped on a narrow bed in the dome laboratory, all the sensations reaching my brain through the robot told me I was on the planet's surface.

As light patterns entered the robot's four video lenses, they were translated digitally and became electrical impulses that followed the electronic circuitry into the robot's computer drive. From there, they were translated into X-ray waves that traveled to the receiver above. The receiver then beamed to the wires of my jumpsuit, which were connected to the antenna plug in my spine. The electrical impulses moved instantly up the nerves of my spinal column into my brain, where my brain did what it always did when light entered my real eyes and hit the optical nerves that reached into my brain—it translated the light patterns into images.

The same thing happened with sound, except of course, with sound waves that usually reached my own ear canals. And with touch. The robot body couldn't taste or smell in the way that humans did, but one of the fingers is wired to perform material testing. All I need are a couple of specks of the material, and this finger will heat up, burn the material, and analyze the contents.

The robot also has heat sensors that detect infrared, so I can see in total darkness. The video lenses' telescoping is powerful enough for me to recognize a person's face from five miles away. But I also can zoom in close on something nearby and look at it as if I were using a microscope.

I can amplify hearing and pick up sounds at higher and lower levels than human hearing. The fibers wired into the titanium let me feel dust falling, if I want to concentrate on that minute level. It also lets me speak easily, just as if I were using a microphone.

The robot is strong too. The titanium hands can grip a steel bar and bend it.

Did I mention it's fast? Its wheels will move three times faster than any human can sprint.

I love controlling this robot body. While my own body is in a wheelchair, this robot gives me the sensation of more freedom than any other human has experienced.

Except today wasn't Mars exploration but maintenance work.

I still didn't mind.

It beat sitting in a wheelchair.

I brought both the robot's titanium hands up in front of a video lens and flexed the fingers, wiggling them to make sure everything worked properly.

I switched to the rear video lens. As promised, the compressed air backpack was in place.

I rolled forward to circle the dome.

Ashley has told me that the sky on Earth is blue and the sun is yellow, but too bright to look at for more than an instant. She tells me clouds are white or, if they hold rain, gray. She says when the sun rises or sets, it stays the same color, but the clouds might turn pink or red or orange or a mixture of all those colors.

On Mars, when the sun rises, it is blue against a butterscotch-colored sky.

A few hours had passed since sunrise, however, and now the sky was red because sunlight scattered through dust particles at a different angle. At sunrise, it had been about -100° Fahrenheit. Now it was 50° above zero. Mars had such radical daily temperature differences because the atmosphere was too thin to hold heat. As soon as the sun set at the end of the day, the planet's heat would bleed back into the cold of outer space.

The 40-mile-an-hour wind and the sand it threw at my titanium shell didn't bother me. With such little atmosphere, even strong winds don't have the force they would on Earth. And the robot body, about the size of a man, was built so tough that it would be standing long after human bodies fell.

I reached the ladder to the dome.

Without hesitation, I grabbed one rung with the titanium fingers of my right hand. I pulled, holding the entire weight of the robot with one arm. I reached for the next rung with my left hand and pulled. One hand after another, I climbed quickly, robot wheels bouncing against the ladder. My arms had such strength that I didn't need to support myself with legs.

It took less than a minute to get to the top of the dome. I

pulled myself onto the platform surrounding the telescope lens.

From there I had an incredible view.

The dome, two stories tall, was made of black glass, hard as a diamond. It stuck out of the Martian plains like a black egg that had been half buried. The dome itself had an area of about four football fields, covering experimental labs, open areas where equipment was maintained, and the mini-domes where each scientist and tekkie lived in privacy from the others. I also saw the dome's greenhouse about a half mile away, where scientists were trying to raise plants that would grow on the planet's surface, even with the lack of oxygen.

As I scanned the horizon, the red mountains, and the brownish red sand of the valley plains, movement on the other side of the greenhouse caught my attention.

Movement?

It was far too small to be a platform buggy on an expedition. Unless it was a tekkie or a scientist in a space suit, there should be nothing moving out there except sand shifted by the wind.

I clicked my forward video lens to get a close-up and nearly jumped out of my robot's titanium shell.

It was another robot. Making circles in the sand.

Another robot?

Impossible.

CHAPTER 6

"Rawling." My voice sounded mechanical since it traveled through a sound-activated communication device attached to the robot body.

"Tyce. You're at the telescope. Need more instructions?" Rawling asked.

I swiveled the robot video lens. The part of the telescope that extended from the dome observatory was like a short tube, twice as wide as the robot's outstretched arms. It rotated on a track railing. Spraying compressed air into the rotational gears would be a simple task.

"No," I said. "Yes."

"No? Yes? Make sense, Tyce."

"No, I do not need instructions on how to clean the gears. Yes, I need advice."

"On what?"

"I am going to switch one of my lenses to the video screen in the lab. You tell me what you see."

"Sure."

I made the switch. I zoomed in even closer and waited for Rawling.

What he would see was a robot body like mine, but different.

I knew what my own robot body looked like, of course.

The lower body is much like my wheelchair. Except that instead of a pair of legs, there is an axle that connects two wheels. The robot's upper body is merely a short, thick, hollow pole that sticks through the axle, with a heavy weight to counterbalance the arms and head. Within this weight is the battery that powers the robot, with wires running up inside the hollow pole.

The upper end of the pole has a crosspiece to which arms are attached. They are able to swing freely without hitting the wheels. Like the rest of the robot, they are made of titanium and jointed like human arms, with one difference. All the joints swivel. The hands, too, are like human hands but with only three fingers and a thumb instead of four fingers and a thumb.

Four video lenses at the top of the pole serve as eyes. One faces forward, one backward, and one to each side.

Three tiny speakers, attached to the underside of the video lenses, play the role of ears, taking sound in. The fourth speaker, on the underside of the video lens that faces forward, produces sound and allows me to make my voice heard.

The computer drive is well protected within the hollow titanium pole that serves as the robot's upper body. Since it is mounted on shock absorbers, the robot can fall 10 feet without shaking the computer drive. This computer drive has a short antenna plug-in at the back of the pole to give and take X-ray signals.

Rawling's whistle of surprise broke the silence around me.

"If I didn't know better, I'd say it was a robot." Rawling's voice, though still calm, was louder in the communication device.

"Me too. And one sleeker than mine."

The robot body I controlled looked bare bones compared to this new one, whose legs, arms, and fingers were sheathed with shiny silver, like metallic skin.

"Tyce," Rawling said into the speakers, "it looks to me like a second-generation robot."

"My guess too," I said. I paused. I didn't want to ask Rawling this question. But I had to do it. "Have you been keeping a secret from me?"

"No," he said a second later. "And as dome director, I should know about this. Which means someone, somewhere has been keeping it secret from both of us."

"That's not good, is it?"

He knew what I meant. The former director of the dome, Blaine Steven, had kept too many secrets. In fact, the last secret he kept nearly killed Rawling and me and my dad during an expedition across the planet. (Mission 3: *Time Bomb* tells that story.)

"No," he said, "that's not good at all."

"Should I try to catch that robot?" I asked.

"Finish your telescope maintenance and get back down as soon as you can."

"But—"

"I'll explain why when you return."

CHAPTER 7

"Tyce, I've pulled up on the computer screen the last 48 hours of activity at the dome entrance."

We had finished three hours of training on the Hammerhead virtual-reality program, and I now sat in Rawling's office. The laboratory where I did the virtual-reality work was very basic—four walls, the bed, the computers. Rawling's office, on the other hand, showed that the previous director had expensive tastes and was not afraid to spoil himself. At $10,000 per pound of cargo, the desk was twice the size of anyone else's in the dome, while the entire office was the size of most mini-domes. There were framed paintings of Earth scenes like sunsets and mountains and a real potted bush in the corner. Rawling kept threatening to get rid of all the stuff because he was embarrassed by all the money it had cost. But on Mars, there was no place to throw it away.

"So who moved that other robot out there?" I asked. It would definitely show on the activity record. There was no other way in or out of the dome.

"Look for yourself."

Rawling turned the computer screen my direction. Digital images of the dome entrance flashed in front of me. It was like entering an igloo with two sealed doors. The outer door remained sealed when the inner door opened. Once the people or cargo moved into the entrance area, the inner door closed and sealed before the outer door opened so that oxygen wouldn't leak out and the dome's pressure wouldn't change. It was a 10-minute process and so important that the entrance was under computerized surveillance all the time.

I kept watching the computer screen. In the lower right-hand corner, digital numbers flicked, recording the time. Rawling was fast forwarding the images so quickly that in less than five minutes, I saw all 48 hours.

"The only robot going outside is mine," I said.

"Exactly. Which is very disturbing. What does that tell you, Tyce?"

I thought it through before I answered. "The robot has been outside longer than 48 hours. Which means if it has been used at all, it should need recharging. But the only source of charging is inside the dome. So either it hasn't been used much, or it doesn't need recharging."

Rawling nodded. "What really scares me is that I reviewed the dome entrance surveillance tapes as far back as they go. One month. That robot did not enter or leave the dome in the entire time. So it's been out beyond the greenhouse, hidden from anyone in the dome for at least a month. And I'd be surprised if today was the only time that robot was active."

"Surprised?" I asked.

"You saw what the other robot was doing. Practice activities. Lifting. Circling. Digging. Practice is just that. Practice. Repeated activities. So what are the chances that the only time someone activated it was while you were on top of the dome?"

"Slim. It would have to be a big coincidence."

"No one but you and I and two tekkies knew you were going up there for maintenance work today. The top of the dome is probably the only place that would give anyone the chance to see the robot. So whoever practices it would have felt safe to use it. I'd say it's much more likely that the robot has been used often and daily." Rawling rubbed his chin. "And that tells us . . ."

I thought again. "First of all, someone else in the dome is running a robot. And second, either the robot has an incredible battery power that doesn't need charging very often, or it has a way of replenishing its power outside of the dome."

"Yes and yes," Rawling said. "But it's something even bigger that bothers me the most."

I knew the answer to that. "You're the director, and you don't know about it."

"Unfortunately, you're right again."

That's why Rawling had told me to finish the telescope maintenance and return to the dome as if we hadn't seen the other robot. Rawling wanted the chance to search for whoever controlled it without that person knowing Rawling was in the middle of a search.

"Tyce, think about what's been happening in the last few months."

Rawling listed the major events since I'd learned to control the robot body. During an oxygen crisis, the former director had tried to save a select few scientists, keeping it secret from the other 180 people under the dome, whom he was willing to let die. Later, we'd discovered that the director had hidden oxygen tanks to help save hybrid animals bred through illegal genetic experiments, rather than saving the 180 dome residents. And recently, the revealing of a supposedly ancient alien civilization had proved there was a conspiracy between a group of dome officials on Mars and a government group on Earth.

"What do all of these have in common?" Rawling asked. He answered his own question. "Secrecy, conspiracy, and ulterior motives at top levels." He shook his head. "I came here as a medical doctor. I was willing to give up 10 or 15 years of my life because I believed—and still believe—that the Mars Project can save millions of Earth lives."

I nodded in agreement. I'd never witnessed the conditions on Earth myself, of course, but I'd been told they weren't the greatest. There was a great threat of overpopulation, and governments were barely holding control as everyone fought for resources. The team's arrival on Mars was Phase 1 of a long-term plan to establish the dome. Phase 2, which my mom had already started, was genetically altering plants that could grow outside the dome so that more oxygen could be added to the atmosphere. The long-range plan—over a hundred years—was to make the entire planet a place for humans to live outside of the dome. If Mars could be made a new colony, then Earth could start shipping people here to live. If not, new wars might begin, and millions of people would die from war or starvation or disease.

"The hope that this dome represents," Rawling continued, "has been enough to keep most of the political powers on Earth working together. It's like a light at the end of the tunnel, even though it's far away and small. But from the few communications I've had, some political leaders on Earth are becoming less willing to work together. So there's a good chance war might break out there soon. . . ." He paused and looked intently at me. "Since I've taken over as director, I've discovered that even though we are 50 million miles from Earth, the politics continue here."

Now I shook my head. "That doesn't make sense, Rawling. I mean, if there is some sort of ongoing conspiracy here at the dome, with a secret circle of people among the scientists, why would the high-level Earth powers put you in the position of director? Wouldn't they want someone from the secret circle in power?"

"I've thought about this long and hard, Tyce. I want to believe some of the high-level people on Earth don't know about the hidden circles here at the dome. And that the ones who *do* want me in position because then it will definitely appear there is no conspiracy. In the meantime, with enough scientists as part of the hidden circle, things can continue the way it used to be under the former director's control."

"Any use in asking him?"

Because of ex-director Blaine Steven's part in the oxygen crisis, then later in the ancient alien civilization hoax, he was in lockup, waiting to be sent back to Earth when the shuttle left again.

"No good at all," Rawling said with a tired smile. "All he has to do is deny any knowledge. And we have no proof."

"Except for the other robot. It didn't get here without someone pulling levers back on Earth."

"Bingo," Rawling said.

"Bingo?"

"Sorry. It's an old Earth expression. A game people played when I was your age."

"What does this 'bingo' have to do with what I said?"

" 'Bingo' means you won."

"I won?"

Rawling sighed. "Forget it. All I meant was that I think

you're right. Someone pulled levers back on Earth to smuggle another robot out here. If I can find out who is behind the other robot, I might be able to learn more about the secret levels of power here at the dome. And if we do that, I'll be able to figure out more about what's happening back on Earth." Rawling sighed again. "And there is that other matter. Remember? A comet that's about to shotgun Mars as target practice."

CHAPTER 8

That night, in the silence that usually fell beneath the dome after the supper hour, when the scientists and tekkies retreated into their mini-domes to read e-books, I followed my own usual habit.

I wheeled across the dome, taking a path on the main level that wound between the dimmed mini-domes. Above me, one level up, a walkway about 10 feet wide circled the inside of the dome walls. People mostly used the walkway for exercise, jogging in circles. They reached the walkway by a set of stairs. I couldn't, of course. So tekkies had built a ramp so I could reach the walkway on a gradual incline. The reason I wanted to get to it was to reach the third and smallest level of the dome, which anyone, including me in a wheelchair, could reach by a narrow inclined catwalk from the second level.

This third level was centered at the very top of the dome and was only 15 feet wide. There, on its deck, a powerful telescope perched beneath a bubble of clear glass that stuck up from the black glass that formed the rest of the dome. From there, the telescope gave me an incredible view of the solar system.

Although I had gone there every night since learning to handle the electronic controls of the telescope as a kid, on this night, like the night before, I didn't want to look through the telescope. To me, the approaching comet was an enemy. It was almost like if I ignored it, it might go away.

No, I had a different reason for heading up to the telescope.

And when I got there five minutes after leaving our mini-dome, that reason was there and waiting for me.

"Let me run an idea past you," I said to Ashley.

I sat near the eyepiece of the telescope. That was one handy thing about being in a wheelchair. You always had a place to sit.

"Sure," she said. She'd pulled up a small bench from the side of the platform and moved it beside me. We both stared downward at the quietness of the dome floor beneath us.

"Remember I've been telling you about the virtual-reality Hammerhead?"

"I'll bet you spent a lot of time today on it," she replied. "Especially after what Rawling announced to everyone at the meeting today."

Rawling had informed all the scientists and tekkies about the approaching comet, then he had promised everyone there was nothing to worry about. He'd told them that a new space torpedo was being prepared to intercept and destroy the comet pieces long before they reached Mars. However, he hadn't told them I would be doing it; he didn't want the extra pressure on me. After all, I was still a kid, and lots of people under the dome still treated me that way.

"At least three hours. Much more than that, and my brain gets too tired."

"Hard work, huh?"

"Hard work," I agreed. "At least today was just a practice run. Without an enemy pilot to face. But tomorrow . . ."

"Back into combat?"

"I know it's just virtual-reality combat, but it's still tough. And that's why I want to run another idea past you."

"Which is . . ."

"I'm going to blow up a moon."

"What?" Ashley lifted her head from looking down at the main level and snapped her eyes onto mine.

"It's just virtual reality, remember? So I won't *really* be blowing up one of Mars' moons."

"But why?" She kept staring at me.

"Simple. I told you before that it's hard to stop in space. I mean, the Hammerhead goes about 15,000 miles an hour. Which means that once you're in front of the enemy space torpedo, you're in big trouble. You can't suddenly slow down and let the other torpedo go by. You stay out in front until finally you get blasted. Even if it is a virtual-reality blast."

"But blowing up a moon?"

"Last time that pilot seemed to come out of nowhere, but I think the space torpedo was hiding by hovering in one of the craters of Phobos. So here's my plan. I'll go past Phobos, just like before. When the torpedo comes out on my tail, I'm going to make a loop back toward the moon. And I'll blast Phobos apart. The lasers are supposed to be that powerful, and Phobos is not near as thick as it is wide. It should be no problem to knock Phobos into a dozen or so chunks."

"I don't get it," Ashley said. "You'll be out of laser power. You'll have nothing left to shoot the other torpedo."

"My gamble is that I won't need to. I should be able to fly through the hole I blast into Phobos. The enemy torpedo will be following so close behind that it's almost certain to get hit by one or more of the chunks of moon caused by the explosion." I shrugged. "It's not much of a gamble. I mean, once you're followed by a space torpedo, you're almost certain to get shot anyway. So why not try something totally unexpected?"

"Might work," she said. "Like you said, it's just a virtual-reality program. In real life you might not want to blow apart a moon."

"Real life," I echoed. "Not to change subjects, but can we talk about Earth?"

"You always want to talk about Earth," she said. She stood from her bench and began pacing the small platform of the telescope area.

"You put me off every time I ask. But this time I want to hear about where you grew up."

Stopping her pacing briefly, she tilted her body left, resting her right hand on her right hip. It was a trademark Ashley pose for when she was annoyed. "What matters is where I am now. Not what happened before. You know I don't like talking about my family life."

That was true. All Ashley had said was that her parents had recently divorced. I didn't know why; it was one thing she found too painful to discuss. Her father was a scientist, and evidently so good that when he'd insisted he wouldn't visit Mars unless he was allowed to take Ashley, he was given permission. No other scientist in the history of the dome had been allowed that privilege.

"You don't have to tell me about your mother," I said.

"That's not what I meant. Remember you told me that you grew up in a place called Denver, Colorado? And how you've told me about the mountains and the lakes?"

"I remember," she said. "It's easy to miss all that when you're on Mars."

"How about if you were born on Mars and have never seen Earth in the first place?"

She smiled for an instant. "Good point."

"Anyway," I continued, "I was trying to learn more about Colorado and Denver, and I tried a search engine on the newspaper files loaded on the mainframe. You forgot to tell me about that tornado a few years back that took out a whole section of the city. That must have been something. I mean, I've read all I can about tornadoes, but I can't imagine what it would be like to go through one. Were you scared?"

"I wish we could talk about something else," she said. It didn't surprise me. Ashley never liked talking about her childhood or her family life.

"Sure," I said. "How about you talk. I'll just listen."

So she began to tell me about her homework assignments.

But I didn't really listen.

I was thinking about something else.

I was thinking about the tornado that had never hit Denver. I had just made that up to see what she would say.

I wondered why she hadn't just told me there was no tornado.

Which made me begin to wonder about a lot of other things.

CHAPTER 9

09.16.2039

Here I am, late at night, clicking my computer keyboard when I should be sleeping. The thing is, thinking about the comet headed for Mars and the destruction it might cause has got me thinking other questions. Especially after I mentioned the tornado to Ashley.

I mean, tornadoes cause destruction too. Maybe not as much as chunks of comet crashing into a planet, but from what I've read about them, they are natural disasters that can hurt or kill hundreds of people at a time. Same with hurricanes, flash floods, earthquakes, monsoons, and even volcano eruptions.

Not long ago, because of the oxygen crisis and my mom's strength even in the face of death, I began to believe in the existence of God. And not only a God "out there," but a God who cares about *me.* You might find it strange, but that belief happened through science. The more I learned about the universe, the harder it was to believe that human life happened by accident. One scientist a long time ago said the chances of that were similar to the chances of blowing up a junkyard and having all the pieces fall together to form a perfectly running high-speed sports car. Lots of other scientists, like my mom, dad, and Rawling, agree. Because of all the details of the universe that had to happen the exact right way at the exact right time, the presence of human life "by accident" on the planet Earth would be like winning the same lottery every week in a row for a year. Pretty low chances.

When you start believing in a Creator and wondering if the universe was actually created for a reason, then you have to start wondering why even further.

And that's where I've been for the last few months. Wondering why—and trying to fit the pieces all together. Why would someone—whom I'm now sure is God—create a universe, and all of us in it? Didn't he have enough to do? Was he bored, and so he decided to create us? Or did he do it because he had some big purpose in mind?

I've also come to believe that I have a soul—a part of me invisible to science and medicine. A part of me that longs for meaning. A part of me that feels love, happiness, hope, and sadness. And then when I realized I had a soul, I wondered why even further.

It's the "why" questions that can drive you nuts.

Like right now. Late at night. Here under the dome. In front of my computer.

If God made us, loves us, and gives us a soul,

why do bad things like tornadoes and hurricanes and volcano eruptions happen to us? Is God a father who lets bad things into the house to hurt his kids—on purpose? Or does God still love us and yet allow bad things to happen sometimes? And if so, why doesn't the bad stuff just happen to bad people, rather than good people? And good things just to good people?

Right now I'm staring at my computer screen, half wanting to smile and half wanting to hit my head against a wall.

It was a lot easier a few months ago, when I didn't ask the "why" questions. Now I think about them constantly. Especially when it's quiet under the dome and an exploding comet is headed directly for Mars.

So I don't have any choice but to think about those questions.

I hope I get *some* sleep tonight.

CHAPTER 10

Hammerhead.

The real Hammerhead.

The next morning Rawling and I stood in front of a storage area near the back of the dome.

The tekkie, a middle-aged man named John Chateau, a French-Canadian who liked to comb his gray hair over a big bald spot on the top of his head, had just opened the door for us.

"Incredible," I said.

The Hammerhead stood on tail fins in a tall, thin crate made of protective plastic tubes. It looked just like the virtual-reality one. The nose of it had flat, wide stabilizer fins that gave it the appearance of a hammerhead shark. Almost hidden at the edges of the stabilizer fins were the holes of dozens of tiny flare nozzles. On the back of the space torpedo, just like a shark fin, was another stabilizer with dozens more tiny flare nozzles. It was black, with the kind of paint that reflected no light. The Hammerhead was only about seven feet tall and maybe double the width of a human body. Just the size of a giant shark.

John nodded with enthusiasm. "Tell you what, kid, this

storage area was declared off-limits to all tekkies. I didn't even know what was in here until yesterday. As a telescope man, I sure wish I could use this to go into outer space instead."

Rawling had explained to me that he didn't know the Hammerhead was at the dome until receiving an encrypted message from Earth a week earlier. In other words, it was just one more secret that Blaine Steven, the former director, had kept from the rest of us.

"It may look like a rocket ship, but it's the most sophisticated robot in the history of mankind," John said. He looked directly at me. "Computer-wise, it has all the functions of the robot you control. But what a difference in appearance, huh?"

"Incredible," I repeated.

"Let me tell you about this baby," John continued quickly, as if he were a little kid proud of his first go-cart. "Most space vehicles need huge rockets and thrusters to be able to escape the gravity of a planet. Huge rockets and thrusters need huge fuel tanks. Nearly 90 percent of the bulk of a vehicle is needed just for that. It doesn't leave much for the actual travel out in space." John reached through the plastic slats and patted the Hammerhead. "This baby is small enough that it is launched from space. Yep, we take it up in a shuttle. That means all of its fuel is there for space travel. And you notice how small it is. That's because it only has room for the onboard computers and one pilot in a space suit. Once again it cuts back the need for extra fuel. Think of it this way. No extra weight or waste is put into it for life support. The space suit already has it. A person can live three days on the surface of Mars in a space suit. So a person can live three days in this thing." He paused. "Of course, no one expects a pilot to be in there that long. The Hammerhead was built for high-speed missions. Like a race car, not a motor home."

"It will really go 15,000 miles an hour?" I asked.

"More. Far more." John was as proud of it as if he had designed it himself. "When you throw a rock here in the dome, it accelerates with the initial force. Then gravity and the friction of air slow it down. In space there's no gravity. No friction. If you throw a rock in space, it will never lose that initial acceleration. The nozzles of the Hammerhead are extremely efficient. They compress the fuel burning and create tremendous pushing power. Whatever force you apply with this in outer space keeps accelerating. Think of it like a rock that gains speed as you drop it from a tall building. Say you're already at 15,000 miles per hour. If you gun it with another burst of nozzle flares, it will accelerate another 15,000 miles per hour and keep that speed of 30,000 miles per hour."

"And so on?" I asked.

"Yep! There's nothing to slow it down, ever, except reverse nozzle thrusts. The only limitations you have are fuel limitations. I believe—" he cupped his face with his right hand and stared thoughtfully past Rawling and me—"if you accelerated this until all your fuel was gone, you'd be at roughly 1.5 million miles per hour." He laughed. "Not that anyone would ever want to do that. And, of course, you wouldn't be able to find a way to stop. Unless you ran into something."

Very funny, I thought. He wouldn't be the pilot. As Rawling had told me a dozen times, the Hammerhead had been designed to be flown by someone with virtual-reality skills and the bio-implant in the spine to translate those skills into actual flight. Even if I would be doing it by remote, running into something wasn't a pleasant thought.

"You are certainly knowledgeable about this," Rawling said to John. "Especially for someone who didn't even know about the existence of the Hammerhead until yesterday."

John beamed. "Thank you. It helped that I was able to spend most of last evening going through the technical manual on it. I'm going to be the one helping Dr. Jordan. He's the expert who helped design and test this back on Earth."

Dr. Jordan. Ashley's father. Strange that he'd kept this a secret so long. And that Ashley, if she did know about it, hadn't mentioned it to me.

Or maybe it wasn't so strange. She did seem secretive at times about anything that happened back on Earth.

But I didn't have time to dwell on my thoughts now.

"One thing," Rawling said thoughtfully. "You mentioned a pilot in a space suit. I understood from the Science Agency's last communication that Tyce would handle this the same way he handles the robot. By remote. Why would there be a need for a pilot on board?"

John frowned. "Then someone yanked your chain, Dr. McTigre. There's no possible way to pilot this except by having someone on board. I mean, the range of this ship far exceeds any remote. And what happens if the ship gets on the other side of a planet like Mars? No remote is going to be able to send or receive information."

"You're telling me," Rawling said slowly, "that Tyce is actually going to be *inside* this space torpedo?"

"No other way," John answered. "Why did you think otherwise?"

"Dr. Jordan didn't once tell me that," Rawling said, angry. "He implied that Tyce would fly it the same way he handles the robot. It's one thing to let Tyce try new technology, and another to make him a guinea pig."

"Look," John said, "Dr. Jordan headed a team of Earth scientists who designed this specifically for a pilot like Tyce. And now we're facing that killer comet. If Tyce doesn't fly it, who will? And if no one flies it, what happens to the dome?"

Rawling didn't say anything else. Because we all knew the answers—but didn't want to hear them.

Back in the lab, Rawling shook his head slowly from side to side.

"I don't know about this," he said.

"Is there a choice?" I asked. "Would you rather I get killed in the dome when the comet pieces hit Mars? Or would you like to give me a chance to save myself and everyone else?"

"I don't know if there's a choice," he answered. "And I'm angry about it. I'm angry that no one told me about the comet until a week ago. I'm angry that no one told me that Dr. Jordan was part of this. I'm angry that until a week ago I didn't even know the Hammerhead existed under this dome." He rubbed his eyes. "And I'm angry that there's probably a hundred other things that have been kept from me." He gave me a tight smile. "I'm so angry now that I'm even more determined to stay as director and get to the bottom of all this."

"Good," I said. "Me too."

I had some questions of my own, and I hoped they'd be answered during today's flight simulation program.

Rawling stared off into space briefly, then sighed. "Well, let's get to business."

Rawling pushed me in my wheelchair over to the bed. He lifted me onto the bed.

"Virtual reality today. That's all. You're not really going to be in space. You're going to be part of a computer program test run. Remember that. Tonight we talk to your parents about the real thing."

Sure, I thought as he strapped me into position. *And when we talk to my parents, they'll come to the same conclusion: as much as they hate the idea of putting my life in danger, there's really no choice. I'll have to go out into the space beyond Mars in a tube barely longer and wider than my body. A tube that travels up to 1.5 million miles per hour. And if I mess up, everyone on Mars and maybe everyone on Earth will die. Talk about pressure.*

We went through the checklist without our usual joking around. Rawling adjusted the blindfold over my eyes and the headset over my ears.

Soon everything around me was dark. I was left alone with all my scary thoughts.

Somehow virtual reality wasn't fun anymore.

Then I began to fall and fall and fall into the deep, deep black . . .

CHAPTER 11

Silence. Monstrously thick silence.

And no sense of motion.

Rawling tells me that on Earth, when you're in a car speeding down the highway, fence posts will snap past you, one by one, in a blur of speed that is both frightening and exciting. In space, however, the stars are at such vast distances that you can't judge your speed in relation to their movement. That's because there is none. Even the sun—a white, glaring ball of fire that looks like it's in your back pocket—is 150 million miles from Mars.

Even worse, you feel no sense of weight—except during acceleration or deceleration. When you are cruising at over 15,000 miles an hour, you feel nothing but the beating of your heart. And all around you, it is velvety black, broken only by stars.

That kind of aloneness is frightening.

I switched from human visual and human audio to the onboard computer receptors.

And in the blink of an eye, it seemed I had been thrown into a crazed pinball machine.

Heat radar showed an approaching space torpedo coming in from my lower right. That radar then coordinated with signals bounced off the face of Mars to give me speed and location readings. I was already at 30,000 miles per hour, with impact radar warning me of harmless space dust. Then a clanging alert told me Phobos was one minute away— only 500 miles.

So this is the situation I've been given in today's combat program, I thought, grinning. I had less than 30 seconds to make a decision.

But I'd already decided much earlier what I'd do. It was something I'd only talked about with Ashley.

I flashed the surface of Phobos with my locator laser. At 300 miles, the laser pocked the small moon like a white dart. Yet I knew that in the blackness of outer space, the white target circle would have appeared like a neon billboard to the other pilot in this flight simulation program.

Twenty seconds to impact.

I kept the white laser circle steady at the center of the moon. It was only 18 miles wide, but at 200 miles away, it was starting to fill my visual.

My impact radars went into high alert.

Fifteen seconds.

I held off on the red laser beam that would destroy the moon.

Twelve seconds.

Ten.

In the remaining eight seconds, I did something that takes far longer to describe than accomplish.

I rolled the Hammerhead hard left, taking a line that would almost scrape the side of the moon with my space torpedo. I vented all my flares, then shut down. Just as I'd done the first time I'd taken the Hammerhead into virtual-reality combat.

A heat mushroom would have filled the other pilot's radar. And, just as before, I coasted out of that heat mushroom. Invisible and untrackable.

Only this time my own heat radar showed that the pilot had fallen for my trick. The heat tracks of the other torpedo had peeled off from Phobos and it had slowed, as if it was going to give Phobos a wide circle and wait for me to show up again.

As if that pilot expected me to blow Phobos into little chunks of asteroid. And there is only one person in this universe who might have had that expectation, I realized.

I drifted for another 30 seconds. Just before peeling away from Phobos, I'd rolled hard enough so that my newly accelerated path would curve me back toward Mars. Actually, between Mars and the space torpedo that waited for me on the other side of Phobos.

That meant when I reignited, this time it would be me behind the other torpedo. I'd be in a perfect position to chase and destroy it.

Which I did, firing my virtual-reality laser weapon with perfect timing.

The heat mushroom of the exploding space torpedo seemed to fill my whole radar screen. Just like my smile filled my entire face.

CHAPTER 12

"Let me tell you what I don't like," my dad said with an edge to his tone.

Dad, Mom, Rawling, and I sat in the common area of our mini-dome. Rawling had just explained to them what we'd learned today about the Hammerhead. That it was actually real—and present on Mars.

"First, it bothers me that I piloted the shuttle here with a cargo list that was false." Dad continued, his dark blond hair waving angrily with each gesture. "Only someone high up in the military on Earth would have the kind of pull to get away with that." He frowned, and his square face looked fierce. "I don't like being messed with by those clowns."

Mom smiled at him. "Honey, don't bottle up your emotions. It could give you ulcers."

While I didn't get my looks from her—she was tall and thin with dark hair and a beautiful face—I definitely got my sense of sarcasm from her.

Normally her teasing worked, and Dad lightened up. Tonight he ignored her comment. That's when I knew he was really bugged—and that he, too, believed some sort of conspiracy was going on.

"Second," Dad said, "I can't believe they shipped it here secretly just for the comet."

Rawling, always a good listener, leaned forward.

"For starters," Dad explained, "you know it takes six months to get from Earth to here."

Yet it took three years for each shuttle to arrive. The reason was that pilots had to wait until the planetary orbits were close together. Planned right, the trip was only 50 million miles. But if a ship left Mars just as Earth was headed to the opposite side of its orbit, the trip would take double the time. So much of the three-year trip meant waiting either on Earth or on Mars. Dad would be leaving again soon, and I wouldn't see him for another three years. It was something I didn't want to think about.

"What I want to know, then," Dad insisted, "is how the military people on Earth knew about the comet ahead of time. If I understand your explanations, Rawling, comets in the far reaches of the solar system are next to invisible until they get close to Saturn. At best, we only have two months' notice of its arrival past Mars. Yet the Hammerhead was sent on a shuttle nearly eight months ago. Did someone on Earth know 10 months ago that the comet would be a threat? And if so, why wait this long to warn us? And why ship the Hammerhead secretly?"

"Maybe," Mom said, "the Science Agency authorities didn't want people on Earth to panic. From all the reports, things are politically unstable. Maybe news of a killer comet would upset the balance."

Mom and Dad both stared at Rawling.

"I'm afraid I can't answer those kinds of questions," he said. "And believe me, I'm as frustrated as you are. I'm director of this dome. I should know about everything. And I wasn't informed about the comet—or the Hammerhead—

until last week when Tyce began his training on the computer program. And let me point out that it must have taken at least a couple of years on Earth for the scientists to develop the flight simulation computer program, and even more time to build the Hammerhead. My gut feeling is that once they knew Tyce's operation let him handle virtual reality directly through his nervous system, they began work on the Hammerhead. And that was when Tyce was only six or seven years old!"

Dad stood. He crossed his arms as he stared down at Rawling. "When they started this program is the least of my concerns. What I'm really worried about is how little training he'll get with the Hammerhead before he heads out into space in a cigar tube!"

Rawling stood too. He didn't back down from Dad's glare. "I care about Tyce as much as you do."

Mom got up quickly and pushed them apart. "Do you two have any idea what's happening here? You're both angry, and you're both looking to fight back against what's making you mad. Except you can't, because the people behind this aren't here. You two are friends. Don't let this destroy that. Especially when now is the time all of us have to work together."

Dad kept glaring at Rawling. "I'm not going to kiss and make up with someone that ugly."

Rawling glared back. "Think I'd let anyone with breath as bad as yours even get close?"

Then they both grinned.

Mom sighed. "Men."

She sat beside me and rested her hand on my arm. I patted her hand.

"I'm learning fast, Dad," I said. "By the time the comet

arrives in two months I don't think I'll have any problems with maneuvering the Hammerhead."

Now it was Rawling's turn to sigh. "This is the part I really hate to bring to all of you."

"Yes?" Mom's hand tightened on the muscles of my forearm.

"I just received another communication from Earth. They say that the Hammerhead's weapon system is going to need testing. If we don't do it now, we won't know whether it'll be effective when the comet is near."

"So when is Tyce going up?" Dad demanded.

"Tomorrow," Rawling said. "A small asteroid is making a loop that will come within five million miles of Mars."

"Five million miles!" Mom exclaimed. "This isn't like sending someone to the store for milk and bread."

"No," Rawling answered. "It isn't. And I wish I could see some way around it. But that asteroid is the only one that will be close enough in the next two months to test the Hammerhead."

He eyeballed Dad. "I'm hoping you can take Tyce into orbit sometime in the afternoon. He'll have to make his first real run in the Hammerhead then."

CHAPTER 13

Normally I was asleep by 11:00. Normally I'd read from an e-book until I fell asleep.

Normally, though, I wouldn't wake up the next day to face the prospect of buckling myself into a thin tube of metal and traveling a couple of million miles. Alone. In an experimental space vehicle.

And normally I wouldn't be filled with sadness and anger. But I couldn't help but go over it again and again. It seemed like my best friend had betrayed me. Who else but Ashley knew that I was going to go into the flight simulation program and blow up the moon as a way to defeat the other pilot? Who else would have pulled away as I approached the moon?

But if it was Ashley, that led to a bunch of other questions. How had she become part of the flight simulation? Why keep it secret?

So I didn't sleep.

At three in the morning, after staring at the ceiling of the mini-dome all night, I lifted myself out of bed and into my wheelchair.

I was restless. Too restless to go to my computer and make diary entries.

So I silently rolled out of my room, out of our mini-dome, and into the hush of the big dome.

The only sound was the gentle, distant *whoosh* of the air circulation pumps. It was dim, with most of the lights turned down. All of the other mini-domes were in shadow.

I just had to talk to Ashley. But wondered if I'd have the courage to knock on her mini-dome when I got there. Especially at three in the morning.

I rolled forward farther in the silence and dimness.

Halfway to the other mini-dome, I heard a strange whirring noise. It was barely noticeable above the air circulation pumps.

Maneuvering my wheelchair backward, I hid beside another mini-dome. I froze and waited.

The whirring noise grew louder.

Seconds later, I discovered what it was.

A robot.

The high-tech one I'd seen the day I was outside the dome.

I followed.

I guessed that the newer-model robot had video lenses to give it four-directional visuals. And that it could also sense my body heat. So I let it move down the path, well out of sight, before I rolled after it, keeping it in range by listening for the whirring of its motor.

I didn't have to follow far. Partly because the entire dome is a circle only 400 yards in diameter. And partly because the robot stopped almost immediately once it passed all the mini-domes and reached the storage areas.

Slowly I rolled to the shadows at the edge of the last mini-dome and peered around the corner.

The robot stood in front of the locked room that held the Hammerhead. One of its sleek titanium arms reached toward the door handle. The titanium fingers gripped the handle and sheared it off.

I gasped quietly. I could tell this new robot had strength that doubled or tripled my own robot's.

The door swung open.

At this time of night, I knew the robot meant to damage the Hammerhead. But what could I do? If I went to get help, what might the robot do in the few minutes I was gone?

And yet there was no way I could sneak up on it. Not if it had infrared sensors like my own robot.

I leaped to a decision and rolled my wheelchair forward.

The robot must have sensed my body heat. Halfway across the short space between the storage area and the mini-domes, I watched it turn toward me. Even in the dim light, its silver skin gleamed.

"No closer," it said quietly.

I had expected the odd monotone of synthetic vocal cords, like on my robot. But this one sounded very human.

I did not stop.

"Human, you are in peril of your life."

I did not stop.

"Turn around, human."

I finally did stop, but I didn't turn around. I was only a few steps from the robot. Like mine, it was the height of a full-grown man, so I had to lean my head back to see straight into its forward video lens.

"Leave the Hammerhead alone," I told it. "Or I will disable you."

I knew where to disable the robot. Or at least I hoped I

knew where. Although it was a second-generation robot, I doubted the power source would be much different than mine—at the back, near the connection to its wheels. A simple tug on a main wire would disconnect the power from the robot's battery pack.

"Go away," it said.

Instead, I rolled the last short distance between us.

In one swift move, the robot's left hand reached out and grabbed my throat. The titanium fingers tightened slightly, enough to keep me from speaking, but not enough to choke me completely. I knew it had the strength to rip my head from my body.

This was my gamble. That I had it figured out right. That only one person under this dome was young enough to have had an operation to let her handle this robot by remote. If I was wrong, the robot hand around my throat would squeeze the life out of me.

"Human, this is your last chance. Blink twice to tell me you will leave."

I blinked twice.

The robot hand dropped from my throat.

I was able to speak again.

"I will leave," I said, "but only if you agree to meet me at the telescope. In five minutes."

"Not possible, human."

"Knock off this 'human' stuff," I said. "You know my name. Just like I know yours."

Its hand reached for my throat again. I put up my arms, one on each side of my throat, so that its fingers couldn't reach all the way around.

"Listen," I said, "I don't know what your game is. But if you want to stop me from disconnecting your power, you're going to have to kill me. And if you decide not to kill me, meet me at the telescope in five minutes."

I continued to stare into the unblinking eye of the video lens.

Finally that large titanium hand with its powerful, deadly fingers dropped.

In an instant, I rolled behind the robot and yanked loose its power cord.

CHAPTER 14

"Hello, Ashley," I said in a reserved tone when I rolled the final few feet onto the platform. "Nice that we could meet."

So it *had* been her handling the robot.

She sat on the bench at the side of the telescope. Now she leaned forward, her elbows on her knees. Shadows hid her face. Above us, through the small, clear-glass bubble, a million stars sprinkled the universe. Below us, the main level of the dome was completely quiet.

"Hello, Tyce. I expected you'd try to talk to me a lot earlier. Like maybe right after we finished the flight simulator program."

"Like right after I blew your torpedo into tiny bits of space garbage."

"Something like that." She let out a long breath. "You knew back then, didn't you? When you told me that you were going to try blasting the moon as a way to get the other pilot?"

"No. When I told you that, I was only guessing. I only knew for sure when the other pilot stopped following and waited for Phobos to explode. You're the only person who could have known I was going to try it. Just like you're the only person who knew I was going to try the heat-vent trick the time before. Only in the first combat mission, I still trusted you."

I rolled beside her and pointed at a small pack on her back. "The new computer remote?"

She nodded. "Wired into my plug. I can go anywhere with it."

"How handy. I guess I'm using ancient technology. I need to be strapped to a bed." I rolled away from her and stared up at the cold stars.

"How did you figure it out?" she asked.

I didn't answer. I was too sad. Too bitter.

I did, however, have a long list of reasons. A while back, she'd asked if I was ready to go to Jupiter. She was half joking, but how could she have known unless she already knew about the Hammerhead? Then, of course, there was the fact that in my first combat mission, the other pilot knew I'd come out of a heat mushroom invisible, with no power. Discovering there was another robot, though, had made me first wonder about her. No one else at the dome could have been young enough for a plug implant. By the time a person is more than five years old, the spine and nervous system have grown too much to make the biological implant work.

"How?" I asked her.

She knew what I meant. "Dr. Jordan." She stopped, then started again. "I mean, my father. He designed the program. It was no problem for him to access the mainframe computer and plug me into it during the times you were scheduled for flight simulation combat operations."

"Why? Why keep it a secret?"

"I wish I could tell you why I'm here," she said. "But I can't."

That wasn't the question I was asking. But since she took it that way, I continued. "Why are you practicing in a second-generation robot? Why is it such a secret? Who is forcing you to keep it a secret? We could have been working together every day."

That's what hurt the worst. She'd been here a couple of months. We'd become friends. Great friends. All along she'd let me talk about my robot. When we'd first met, I'd been in the robot body, and she'd pretended not to know how it worked. I wondered how much else of our friendship was a lie.

Tears shimmered in her eyes. "Tyce, I can't answer any of those questions." She let out another breath.

"Can't? Or won't?"

She hesitated a long time. "Won't."

"I was dumb to think we were friends," I said angrily.

"Tyce, I can't tell you. It would hurt too many others. Even that is saying too much. I don't know how to make you understand that."

I felt so betrayed that I wanted to lash out at her. But I couldn't turn in my wheelchair and swing a fist at her. So I turned my head and used words. "You've talked to me for hours about how you believe in God and how you want to follow Jesus and his teachings. I can see you really mean that now."

Ashley had once given me one of her silver earrings. In the shape of a cross. It hung around my neck on a thin, silver chain. I lifted it off my neck and held it out.

"Take this back," I said. "It doesn't mean anything to me."

I got a gasp of pain from her, and I still didn't stop. "That was cheap, you know, what you did in that first combat mission, setting me up with the heat-vent trick. You could have at least made the combat missions a fair fight."

I threw the silver chain and cross at her. She caught it and stared at it.

"I didn't blow you up in that first combat," she said quietly. "I had a chance but didn't. Remember?"

"All I remember," I said, gritting my teeth, "is that we talked about the heat-vent trick and you used it against me. Let me repeat, I was set up."

"Like you did when you set me up on the second combat mission? Why else tell me you were going to blow up Phobos, and then fake it during flight simulation?"

"I only did that," I said, "because I wondered if you were the other pilot. It proved you were. And it proved you are a backstabbing liar."

I heard a muffled sound. It took a second to figure it out.

Ashley was crying. She held her face in her hands and choked back the sobs. Her shoulders heaved. Her words came out in ragged gasps. "Tyce, I had to win so I'd be the test pilot tomorrow. You didn't know it was a contest, and . . ."

She had to fight for breath, but her tears didn't make me feel sorry for her. Because of one simple thing. What I'd seen only minutes earlier down on the main level.

"And when you didn't win, you decided to wreck the Hammerhead so I couldn't fly. That's why you sent your robot there. To spoil what you couldn't have."

She spoke as if she were now gritting her teeth in great pain. "You . . . don't . . . understand. . . ."

"Then make me understand." I said coldly, facing her again.

"I needed to be the pilot. Because I know why they want it tested. And I have to stop them."

"Stop them?" I demanded. "Who is them? What needs to be stopped?"

"Tyce—"

A voice from below interrupted us. "Ashley? Ashley?"

Dr. Jordan. Her father. Calling softly so that scientists and tekkies wouldn't be disturbed.

Ashley sat upright, as if she'd been shot. "He can't know we've talked!"

"Make me understand," I said coldly, "or I'll call him up here right now."

She walked the short space between us. Dropping to her knees at the side of my wheelchair, she pleaded, "Tyce, please. Help me. Telling you what I know could cost me my life."

"No," I said. "You made the problem. You deal with it."

His voice drifted up to us again. "Ashley? Ashley?"

She gripped my arm. I pulled it away.

"Tyce, please. Yes, call him up here. But let me get away first so I'll have time to reconnect the power supply to the robot. He can't know I moved it. This is a life-or-death thing."

"Ashley?" her father continued to call. "Ashley?"

She gripped my arm again.

"I think I'll let him keep wandering until he finds the robot," I said. "Unless you have a few things you'd like to tell me."

"There's a simple glitch in the programming of the telescope's computer. You can fix it easily. Only don't let anyone know you've fixed it, because then Dr. Jordan will realize I've told you. Fix it, then look for the comet. If you don't see it, miss your targets tomorrow on the test run. That's why I wanted to be the pilot. Hitting those targets will kill millions on Earth. Believe me. Millions. And they're set up to do that on this mission."

"Ashley? Ashley?" His voice was directly beneath us.

How did she know this? Why hadn't she told me earlier?

"Give me one good reason to believe you," I said.

There was a long silence. When she finally spoke again, it was as if someone had pulled a noose tightly around her throat.

"Remember I told you I grew up in Denver."

Yes, I remembered. Asking her about the tornado was just one more clue that she'd lied to me.

"I didn't," she whispered. "That's what I'm supposed to tell everyone. Just like I'm supposed to tell everyone that Dr. Jordan is a quantum physicist. He's not. He's an expert in artificial intelligence. And more."

"More?"

She ignored answering my question. "When I met you, I just wanted to be friends. I should have known from the beginning all of this would happen."

Everything she told me just led to more questions.

"I still haven't heard a good reason to believe you," I said.

"Please. Give me a chance to get back down to the main level," she said softly. "Then call him up here. Delay him as long as you can so I can move the robot. There are others. Like us. And we are their only hope."

She placed the silver chain and cross on my lap.

Then she ran.

CHAPTER 15

Dr. Jordan reached the telescope platform five minutes later. He scowled down at me.

I hadn't seen much of him since he'd arrived on the last shuttle. Just glimpses as he hurried from one mini-dome to another.

His face was round, like his gold-rimmed glasses. His goatee was round too, and his nose was turned up at the end, showing the dark of his nostrils as two more circles.

To me, the strange thing was that Ashley didn't look anything at all like him. Ashley hated talking about her family. All she'd ever said was that her father and mother had divorced. Maybe Ashley looked a lot more like her mother. Or maybe Ashley was even adopted. Whatever it was, it didn't seem like Ashley was able to get along with her father like a friend, which was sad. I was lucky with my parents.

"Is Ashley here?" Dr. Jordan demanded.

I thought it was a dumb question from a scientist who was supposed to be so smart. What did he think—that she was hiding beneath my wheelchair?

"I heard you calling for her," I said. "I was just wondering if she was OK."

His impatience with me turned his scowling mouth into a tight, little circle. I wondered if he knew that about himself—that his face was a bunch of little circles within a larger circle.

"Unless she stepped out of the dome in the middle of the night, of course she's OK."

"But you're looking for her."

"That's her business and mine."

"Well," I said, "I was just wondering if I could help."

"I doubt it," he snapped. Then his irritation turned to brief puzzlement. "What are you doing up here, anyway? You should be getting rest. Tomorrow's your real test run in the Hammerhead."

"I couldn't sleep. So I came up here to look at the stars."

"The telescope isn't functioning."

I pointed to the clear glass of the dome above us. "But my eyes work. It's beautiful, isn't it? The Martian night sky."

"Beauty is only something attributed by sentimental humans," he hissed. "And those stars are simply big balls of hydrogen fusing into helium, throwing off light and heat in the process. What you are looking at is physics. Beauty isn't measurable, so it doesn't exist."

"Oh."

"Good night," he said curtly. "Don't waste my time again. And I advise you to get some sleep."

Sleep?

No. If Ashley was right about the telescope, it wouldn't be difficult to find out. The telescope was computer driven, with a small screen and keyboard beside the eyepiece.

Viewers keyboarded coordinates or the names of stars, planets, or constellations, and the telescope, when it was working, would track the specified object.

Rawling had long ago given me a password to let me enter the system. I knew the basics of computer programming. I entered the system and did some minor hacking. It took some very simple programming and less than five minutes to make the tracking systems operational again. And the telescope hummed on its gears as it swung into action.

An hour later, I was still on the telescope platform, with Dad beside me. His face was pressed against the eyepiece. His hair stuck out in all directions, but at four in the morning, a person should not be expected to look his best.

Dad sat back from the eyepiece and turned his eyes toward me. "I don't see anything," he said. "Where's this great astronomical discovery you promised?"

"My point exactly."

"Tyce, when you woke me up and insisted I come up here at this crazy time, I didn't complain. Sure, I had some questions about why you were out of our mini-dome at this time of night, but when you refused to answer, I trusted you had a good reason. So here I am. Awake when I should be asleep. And you're telling me your great astronomical discovery is nothing?"

"Yes," I said. "In one way, that's the best news you could get."

"Sure," he said, but I knew he didn't mean it. "Tyce, I'm going back to bed before I get mad. Tomorrow we're going to discuss this. When I'll be awake enough to enjoy being mad at you."

"Listen to me, Dad. Don't you find it surprising that the telescope is working again?"

He shrugged. "Not really. I assumed that one of the tekkies fixed it today."

"No," I said. "I did. Half an hour ago. All it took was some simple rewriting of the computer code."

I wondered why the tekkies hadn't been able to figure it out. And why Ashley knew about the computer error. But I'd worry about all of that later. Especially with what I was about to tell Dad.

"So you fixed it." He yawned. "Is that such a big deal that you pull me out of bed?"

"If I waited until morning," I said, "you wouldn't have been able to use the telescope during the daylight. I didn't want to wait until tomorrow night to show you."

He snorted. "Might as well use it during the day. Doesn't make much difference if you're not seeing anything spectacular during the night."

"Dad," I said patiently, "I've got the coordinates of the telescope set up to where the Earth scientists tell us the killer comet is sweeping past Jupiter."

Dad frowned at me. He leaned forward again into the eyepiece of the telescope. He spent 30 seconds squinting. He leaned back. "I don't see it." He shook his head. "You sure you have the right coordinates?"

"I triple checked," I answered.

"But there's no comet."

"And that," I said, "is my big discovery. There is no comet." Some of my trust in Ashley was coming back. If only I could ask her more questions.

"No comet? That doesn't make sense."

"The telescope wasn't working," I said. "Almost as if

somebody wanted us to believe there was a comet and didn't want us to be able to check it out for ourselves."

Dad took a quick look through the eyepiece again. He spoke as he stared out into space. "But, Tyce, why would someone want everyone to believe a deadly comet threatened to hit Mars?"

"That," I said, "is a very, very good question."

CHAPTER 16

The next day, I had wanted to wake earlier than I did so I could talk to Ashley. But I hadn't managed to fall asleep until five in the morning.

When I finally woke up, it was like I entered a coma. Normally, all Mom or Dad has to do is call my name and I wake up. This time, Dad had to shake my shoulders.

"Huh?" I said. I blinked, trying to focus my eyes.

"Two hours until countdown," he answered. "We wanted to let you sleep as long as possible. But Rawling is here and wants to talk."

I swallowed a few times, trying to get moisture in my mouth. I remembered last night's events. "Does he know about the comet?"

Dad nodded. "That's why he's here."

"I'll be right out."

Minutes later I rolled into the common area of our mini-dome.

Rawling had a coffee in his hand. He smiled bleakly at me. "We don't have much time," he said. "I wish I could call off this test run, but I can't. It would go against direct orders from Earth. So we need to talk about a comet that doesn't exist. And about a Hammerhead that does exist but gets shipped here in secrecy. And whatever we talk about, we keep quiet until we figure this out." Sipping his coffee, Rawling made a face. He always complained that he missed Earth coffee more than anything else.

"There's more," I said.

Rawling lifted his eyebrow.

"Ashley. She's the one who handles the other robot."

Rawling set his coffee down and leaned forward, an intense look on his face. "I'd thought the same but had no way of proving it. She's the only other person under the dome young enough to have the bio-implant. How did you find out?"

I told him about my conversation with her the night before.

"Let me get this straight," Rawling said. "Both times you were in the flight simulation combat, she was the other pilot?"

Dad had been listening closely too. He poured a refill of coffee into his cup and offered a refill to Rawling. Rawling took it, sipped, grimaced, and set it down.

"All I can think of," I said, "is that she works with Dr. Jordan the same way you work with me. It wouldn't be difficult for Dr. Jordan to know when you had me scheduled for the flight simulations. All he'd need to do is get into the computer mainframe and link Ashley into it the same way that I do. I mean, the flight simulation is basically a virtual-reality computer game. And in a computer game, you can play the computer or a human opponent, right? All Dr. Jordan needed to do was get Ashley into the game."

"Sure," Rawling said slowly. "But if that's the case, why

wouldn't Dr. Jordan let us know that Ashley was part of this? That's what is driving me crazy. All the secrets here."

"Not just secrets here," Dad corrected. "But secrets from Earth. Let's face it. Someone there is making the decisions to spend the money they did on the Hammerhead. Someone there was able to fake the shipment papers. Someone there sent us the communications about a killer comet. We've been thrown into a game where we don't know the rules."

"We've been thrown into a game without being told the game is happening," Rawling said. "And the biggest question of all is why?"

They had begun to talk to each other like I wasn't there. I had to cough to get their attention. They turned to me.

"I've got a guess," I said. "At least a guess about the reason for the comet and the Hammerhead."

I told them. And I told them when and where I wanted to ask the questions I had about my guess.

I couldn't find Ashley in the last hour before we went into the countdown preparations. I discovered why when I finally gave up looking and wheeled over to the platform buggy that would take us out to the launch site, about two miles from the dome.

Ashley was there. Inside the buggy. With Dad. And Dr. Jordan. She couldn't meet my eyes.

Dr. Jordan did, though. "Ashley's here to observe," Dr. Jordan said to my unspoken question. "Today's an exciting day in space history. I want her to be part of it."

Somehow, Ashley didn't look excited. I thought I knew why. But only the next few hours would let me know if I was right.

stepped inside, and the inner door closed before the outer door opened.

Dad had explained to me earlier that when that outer door opened, the vacuum of outer space sucked smaller, unsecured contents out through the gap like a miniature explosion. Humans in space suits were flexible enough to get sucked out in the first surge. So he had warned me to buckle the safety cable of my space suit to the iron rings set inside the cargo bay. If I tumbled out, I'd go with so much speed that the chances of any space vehicle finding me out in space were next to impossible. I'd be doomed to a slow death, floating in space as I waited for my oxygen and water to finally run out.

Dad floated behind me as I punched the button to open the inner cargo door. We'd worked it out beforehand. He would enter the cargo bay with me and help me into the Hammerhead. Once I was secured inside the space torpedo, he would reenter the Habitat Lander, close the inner door again, and finally open the outer door to set the Hammerhead free. He, Dr. Jordan, and Ashley would be able to watch from the observatory window.

Out here in space, time seemed not to exist. Our slow, weightless movements felt eerie.

We waited until the inner door slid open, and Dad followed me into the cargo bay.

"Safety clip," Dad said, pointing at the iron rings. I started to buckle my safety cable in place, and so did he.

"Roger." Someday I was going to ask Dad or Rawling where that phrase came from. Meanwhile, it sounded cool, and so I used it.

Dad fumbled with the catch of the Hammerhead's hatch. When it finally opened, I pulled myself inside.

It was a tight fit, space suit and all.

CHAPTER 17

The launch was routine, or at least as routine as you could expect any time 500,000 horsepower was generated to break several tons of equipment and rocket fuel away from the gravity and atmosphere of a planet.

I wasn't worried anyway.

My dad was the best. He'd shuttled the Habitat Lander between the surface of Mars and the orbiting Crew Transfer Vehicle dozens of times. That was how interplanetary travel worked. The CTV was large and comfortable enough for the six-month journey to Earth. In space, with no air friction or gravity, it didn't matter whether a vehicle weighed two tons or 10. If I'd been able to brace against something, a simple push of my arm would be enough to send the CTV on its way.

But launching a CTV from planetary gravity was a totally different story. It would take megatons of fuel and demand an aerodynamic construction like a rocket ship, limiting the room for crew. So the CTV instead orbited Mars, and the Habitat Lander was used to carry things back and forth from Mars (or Earth, if the CTV was parked there).

The Habitat Lander was much smaller. With Dad as pilot, Dr. Jordan, Ashley, and me—all of us strapped in against the G-force on takeoff and landing—there was barely enough room for the extra space suits. The Hammerhead had been secured in the cargo bay.

No one said much before takeoff. We were all in space suits, but that wasn't the reason for silence. Space suits are all connected by radio, and we could have heard each other easily.

Dad was looking down at his countdown checklist.

Dr. Jordan still looked angry. I'd overheard him yelling at Rawling that morning. He'd been furious that someone had broken the lock to the storage room. I'd seen him check out the Hammerhead at least a dozen times after that, probably making sure it hadn't been tampered with.

Ashley, too, seemed unusually quiet. I hadn't spoken with her since the night before, when we'd been at the telescope. And now she wouldn't even make eye contact with me. I hadn't had a chance to tell her that I hadn't ratted her out. Instead, I'd calmly invited Dr. Jordan to look at the stars with me when he made it up to the telescope. I hadn't had a chance to tell her that he had hissed impatiently at me. And then he stomped away, complaining about wasted time.

I didn't have much to say. At least not yet. I was angry, too, but for a very different reason.

Just then the rockets roared. The Habitat Lander shook hard, as if Mars were a giant dog reluctant to let it go. A minute later we broke from the planet and shot through the air. G-force flattened my face.

This was my first trip into space. I should have been enjoying it. I should have been excited about getting into orbit and seeing Mars for the first time the way I'd been seeing it in the virtual-reality computer programs.

But I didn't enjoy the trip. Like Ashley, I'd lost a lot of my excitement.

CHAPTER 18

Once we were in orbit, getting into the Hammerhead was relatively simple.

I was already in my space suit. That part had been awkward on Mars because of the low gravity. Dad had helped push my legs inside.

Here in orbit, however, it didn't matter that I couldn't use my legs. Moving was as easy as pushing off with a finger or elbow. Any other time I would have loved that freedom. But I had to focus on what I needed to do, so I didn't even look out through the observatory windows at Mars.

"Right behind you, Tyce," Dad said into his space suit radio when I reached the sealed doors that led to the cargo bay. "Remember the space pilot's first rule. If for any reason you think it's unsafe to proceed, you can abort the flight. This isn't about trying to be brave."

"Roger," I said, knowing Ashley and Dr. Jordan were on the same channel.

The cargo bay doors worked on the same principle as the entrance to the dome. When the inner door opened, some of the air from the ship filled the cargo bay. Yo

Only once I was inside, with the hatch still open, did Dad unclip my safety cable. The end of it retracted, following me into the Hammerhead.

"Everything still fine, Son?"

"Roger."

Dad secured the hatch. "I'm not leaving the cargo area until you hook yourself up to the onboard computer. Remember the space pilot's first rule. If for any reason—"

I grinned and finished his words. "—I think it's unsafe to proceed, I have the right to abort the flight."

It took me five minutes to get the onboard computer ready. My plug had already been attached to an antenna wired into my space suit. It traded signals with the Hammerhead's onboard computer, and when they had finished talking to each other, everything was ready.

There was a small observatory port in the Hammerhead.

I lifted an arm to give Dad a thumbs-up.

He saw it and nodded. "Run through your checklist with me," he said.

I did.

"You're ready, Son," he said. "The Hammerhead is hooked by a safety cable to the inside of this cargo bay. When the outer door opens, you get pulled out 20 or 30 yards. I will repeat that the pilot—you—has the control switch to release that safety cable. In other words, the flight is your decision. Because remember the first rule of space pilot safety. If for any reason—"

"Dad, I'm fine."

He rapped on the observation panel of the Hammerhead. "I'm proud of you, Son. I love you." With those words, he pushed away.

Thirty seconds later, with the inner door sealed and Dad safely inside the Habitat Lander, the outer cargo door slid open. The Hammerhead bumped against the opening doors as the explosion of pressure shot through the gap. As the doors opened fully, it bobbed out of the cargo bay completely. It stopped at the end of the cable.

The Habitat Lander loomed large in my observation window. I could see Dad and Dr. Jordan at the Lander's window.

All that held me to the safety of the orbiting Lander was a thin, steel cable.

When I released it, I would be all alone in space.

I shivered.

CHAPTER 19

Incredible.

I floated in total, peaceful silence. By turning my head, I saw the edge of Mars. It was so large against the black backdrop of space that all I could see was a small part of the red planet's curve and its shimmering atmosphere. In the distance were rings of craters and lines of mountain ranges. And when I lifted my eyes, I could see beyond the curve, to where a bright blue ball, swirled with white, hung motionless. Earth.

Tears filled my eyes at this beauty.

I wondered if heaven would be anything like this. Total peace. A sense of total freedom. And an overwhelming sense of awe of the God who created all of this.

"Tyce." Dr. Jordan's brisk voice broke into my thoughts.

"Yes, Dr. Jordan."

"You haven't begun countdown. Do you have any questions before you begin?"

All I had to do was instruct the onboard computer to begin the preignition countdown. Once the rocket flares ignited, the Hammerhead would be mine, responding instantly to my thoughts. I'd be able to race through space.

I'd be able to explore a million miles as easily as rolling my wheelchair along a path. I'd be able to flit among the moons of Mars, cruise above the planet, head for the asteroids.

But I had questions.

"Yes?" Dr. Jordan sounded impatient.

"I do have several questions, sir."

"Please make them brief. You are familiar with all the controls. The Hammerhead is fully prepared and ready."

"Yes, sir."

I looked at Earth again. Thought of all the lives on that planet. Thought of mothers, fathers, and their kids. Wondered what it would be like to be destroyed in a single burst of red from a space torpedo that circled the Earth.

"Tyce! Your questions?" Dr. Jordan's irritated voice rang in my helmet.

"Sir, this laser that I'm going to use on an asteroid. It has a range of 3,000 miles, correct?"

"Yes, we've been through that. Fire from extreme range to ensure you do not endanger the Hammerhead with asteroid fragments. It is a prototype, worth approximately 15 billion dollars."

"No one has tested this weapon before, sir?"

"Of course not. Which is why you are going on this mission today." Dr. Jordan didn't bother to disguise his sigh at my stupidity.

"But, sir, wouldn't a test like this break all of the nontesting treaties set up by the United Nations? I mean, hasn't there been a ban on any new weapons testing since 2010?"

"Tyce, a comet is two months away from destroying Mars. In these circumstances, today is not a weapons test. It is preparation for the prevention of catastrophe."

Every time I said the word *sir,* I bit it off. Cold and short.

Because I was getting angrier and angrier at what it seemed Dr. Jordan really wanted me to do. And it didn't involve a comet. It was something much, much worse.

"I hope you are finished with these pointless questions."

"Almost, sir."

Another one of his aggravated sighs echoed in my helmet.

I kept my eyes on Earth, 50 million miles away—where all those people were so unaware of this tiny Hammerhead space torpedo.

"Sir, this laser weapon is capable of penetrating a planet's atmosphere," I said slowly.

"Pointless, pointless, pointless," Dr. Jordan muttered.

"Is it, sir? What if I uncabled the Hammerhead and decided to circle Mars and destroy the dome? Is that possible?"

"Your family and friends live beneath that dome. You would not be so insane."

"Sir," I repeated, "does this space torpedo have the capacity to destroy planetary targets?"

There was a long pause. Finally he answered. "In theory, yes."

"Including targets on Earth."

"A ridiculous statement."

"Sir, does this space torpedo have the capacity to destroy targets on Earth?"

My eyes could trace the safety cable. It was barely visible—and my only link to the Habitat Lander.

"In theory, yes," he answered. "But your questions are impertinent. If you don't learn to listen better, you probably won't be given a chance to explore space again."

That was a threat, and I understood it very well. But this was more important than my career as a space pilot.

"Yes, sir," I said. "I'm afraid I have just a few more questions."

The questions that Dad and I and Rawling had discussed in the morning over coffee.

"No," he said, his voice rising. "Begin the countdown."

I gulped and continued. "The earliest any astronomer could have spotted the comet was five months ago. Yet this space torpedo was loaded for shuttle to Mars well before that. Can you explain why?"

He answered immediately. "If you had any brains, you'd realize design work on the Hammerhead would have begun at least 10 years earlier. Obviously then no one knew the comet would appear. So the conclusion is simple. This project was started in anticipation that a comet or asteroid might someday threaten Mars or Earth. It is a timely coincidence that the Hammerhead arrived here when it did."

"A *coincidence?*"

Dr. Jordan evidently caught my tone of disbelief. "Do not forget that, in many ways, the dome is a *military* operation. Insubordination is not an option. Now begin the countdown!"

"Two more questions, sir," I insisted. "One, why is the virtual-reality program set up for pilot combat—if, as you say, the Hammerhead is designed to only fight comets?"

"Begin the countdown!"

"Sir, I believe," I continued stubbornly, "that the Hammerhead is designed as a weapon of war. I believe it will break the weapons ban treaty to test this new laser. I believe once the Hammerhead has proven itself, the military will have the ultimate fighting weapon. And with political unrest on Earth, it will give total dominion to whichever government controls the Hammerhead."

"You are out of line!" Now Dr. Jordan shouted so loudly that my ears hurt.

My dad interrupted. "Jordan, talk to my son civilly. Or speak to me directly."

"Your *son*." It sounded like Dr. Jordan could hardly hold his anger. "Your *son* is out of order."

"Is he?" Dad asked. "Or is he getting close to the truth here?"

Silence.

I filled it. "Sir, I have just one more question."

If I was right, the Hammerhead would truly be unstoppable. It could circle the Earth at speeds unknown to any previous military weapon. With a red burst, it could hit any target, raining horror down from the sky. I was ready for my final question.

"Dr. Jordan, will you please tell me why the telescope was not operational? Why, when it was fixed, I could not find the comet at the coordinates given to Dr. McTigre?"

Rawling is going to find out more about the tekkie responsible for the telescope. It can't be an accident—the fact the telescope wasn't working.

"Mr. Sanders." Dr. Jordan's voice was so furious that it cracked. "Command your son to obey!"

Dad's words came through loud and clear in my helmet. "My son is the pilot. He is in control of the ship. I will respect his decision. As shall you. And I, too, find it very interesting that the comet you say we're targeting does not exist."

I wanted to cheer at the stern anger in Dad's voice.

"Begin the countdown," Dr. Jordan ordered me. "*Immediately.*"

"Are you saying that you have no answer?" I asked. "Or are you saying that the threat of a comet does not exist? Are you saying it's a manufactured excuse so that governments on Earth will not question you as you break the international weapons ban treaty to test the greatest military equipment invented in the history of humankind?"

"Begin the countdown! *Immediately!*" Dr. Jordan was almost screaming.

"Will you answer my questions?"

"I repeat, begin the countdown!" he now yelled full force into my helmet.

"Sir," I said calmly, "might I remind you of the space pilot's first rule?"

"Begin the countdown. Immediately. That is a direct order," he barked.

He didn't sound like a scientist. He sounded like a military general. My hunch had been proven right.

"Sir, I believe it is unsafe to proceed," I said slowly. "I abort this flight."

CHAPTER 20

Fifteen minutes later, I was inside the Habitat Lander. Part of me ached with regret for how badly I had wanted to take the Hammerhead into space. Yet I knew a few moments of freedom outside of my wheelchair compared so little to the terror that the Hammerhead could inflict on Earth, if it was transported back and launched from the moon.

One look at Dr. Jordan's face through his space helmet, and I knew he was furious. His face was puffed with anger. All that showed through his space helmet were his eyes, his nose, and his bared teeth.

He and I both knew he could not force me to fly. No one, not even the highest military general, had the power to make a pilot break the safety rule.

I thought then that I'd won. That even with an hour until our shuttle finished its orbit and was in position to return to Mars, the Hammerhead would not fly.

I was wrong.

"Ashley," Dr. Jordan said a few seconds after I had pushed my way into the crew area, "remember when I told these two you were merely a sightseer, along for the ride?"

"Yes." Her voice was barely audible in our space helmets.

"Now is the time they learn the truth about you. That you, too, are capable as a test pilot."

She nodded very slowly. A glint of silver inside her space visor caught my eye from the earring she wore. The one that matched mine around my neck. Seeing the earring reassured me. I knew what she believed. I could trust her. It was a symbol, too, of our friendship. She wouldn't fly. Not after our conversation on the telescope platform the night before.

"Prepare for a target mission," Dr. Jordan hissed.

"Yes," she said.

"Ashley!" I shouted. "You can't."

She is betraying me again!

"I can," she said. "I can. And I will." She paused. "And I don't want any help in the cargo bay. Not from either of you."

Now it was reversed.

Me in the observation window of the Habitat Lander. Me looking down on the space helmet that showed through the much smaller observation window of the Hammerhead.

The space torpedo was still tethered to the much larger Habitat Lander. It hung in orbit with us. As a backdrop, the giant red surface of Mars moved slowly beneath it.

It could have been me there, ready to explore the space beyond Mars.

But it was Ashley.

And, unlike me, she had begun the preignition countdown.

Tiny flares, each as bright as a sun, suddenly burst from the rocket nozzles of the Hammerhead.

"Excellent, Ashley," Dr. Jordan said. "Now go ahead and release the safety cable."

I could only imagine a click as the Hammerhead released it. The cable floated harmlessly away.

"Thank you, Ashley. You know your mission. Stay in radio contact as long as possible. We will monitor you on radar and with satellite transmitters."

Inside the Hammerhead was the equivalent of a global positioning unit, which would fire radio waves back to a locator on the Habitat Lander.

"Yes," she said. "But I won't make it past Phobos."

"I don't understand," Dr. Jordan said.

"Watch," she replied. "You'll understand soon enough."

The Hammerhead lifted slightly and hovered beside the Habitat Lander's observation window. Through the tiny window of the Hammerhead, I couldn't see Ashley's face—just the dark globe of her space helmet against the lighter background of her space suit.

"Tyce," Ashley said.

"Ashley?"

"Good-bye, my friend. I wish it didn't have to be like this. I wish it could have been different. Remember what I told you at the telescope. Remember the silver earring."

Then the Hammerhead waggled, like fingers waving good-bye.

With a burst of brightness, she and the Hammerhead disappeared into the solar system.

We watched it on radar.

For 3,500 miles the Hammerhead continued to gain

speed on its approach to Phobos, that small moon only 18 miles wide.

The Hammerhead did not swerve.

Twenty seconds before impact, Dr. Jordan began to scream in disbelief.

Ten seconds before impact, I began to pray—with my eyes open. I couldn't pull my eyes away from the radar screen, which showed a tiny fast blip moving toward a bigger, much slower blip.

Five seconds before impact, I moved to the observation window and stared out into the deep black of the solar system.

One second before impact I took a deep breath and said good-bye. By then there was no mistaking Ashley's intent. It takes bulletlike accuracy to hit the only object in space between Mars and the asteroid belt millions of miles away.

Then there was impact.

I heard it through the alarm bell on the radar screen.

And saw it. A bright bloom of light flashed off as quickly as it had flashed on, leaving only the deep darkness of space.

And a deep emptiness in my heart.

CHAPTER 21

Two days had passed since Ashley chose to pilot the Hammerhead into Phobos. For those two days, after arriving back on Mars, I'd been locked in my room, refusing to talk to anyone except Mom and Dad.

I knew everyone under the dome would be in shock. And I didn't want to hear them talk about Ashley being dead. Last night Mom and Dad told me that the new impact bowl on the face of Phobos, easily seen from the dome's telescope, had been named "Ashley's Crater." I'm not sure I'll ever want to go up to the dome's telescope again.

I wonder if anyone on Earth will ever know the price Ashley paid to keep their blue sky a place of safety, not death?

After the "test run," I had arrived home so exhausted that I hadn't even had the strength to put any of my thoughts on my computer. Until now.

It's like what Dad and I just talked about. Every sword always has two edges: a good side, and a dangerous side.

Nuclear fission could be used as a source of

cheap energy. Or it could make a bomb that would destroy entire cities.

Genetic research could save lives with medical advances. Or be used to create hideous new creatures.

The Hammerhead could help us by sweeping away asteroids or comets that threaten human life. Or it could destroy millions of people if military people used it to try to control the universe.

And so on. Every new invention or advance could be used for good. Or not for good.

That was the two-edged sword.

I leaned back in my wheelchair and sighed.

I wished badly that Ashley would step through the doorway and give me a big grin.

I wished badly that she was up at the telescope, waiting for me.

I wished badly that I could have the chance to apologize for what I'd said to her up there the other night. I wished I could tell her that I understood she really lived what she believed. That by sacrificing her life, she had given all she could for others.

Most of all, I wished I could go back in time and let her wreck the Hammerhead with her robot, so that she wouldn't have had to do it the way she did in space.

But I wouldn't have that chance.

All I'd have were memories.

As Dad explained, evil is part of the two-edged sword. Evil exists because God allows us to make choices. He wants us to *choose* to love and obey him, instead of being forced to do what he wants us to do. As humans, sometimes we choose to do good. But other times we choose to do evil. And that's why evil exists, and sometimes bad things happen that are outside our control. Like the fact that Ashley felt she had no other choice than to take the Hammerhead into a direct collision course with Phobos. Otherwise, the Hammerhead could have been used to destroy millions on earth. And like the fact that she had to be so secretive about her past, in order to protect the others she'd talked about. And just who were those "others"? I wondered.

And then Dad and I talked about Ashley's death. I asked him why she had to die so young. Dad said he didn't have an answer for that. And that there were some things we would not know until we got to heaven and could ask God face-to-face. The most important thing, Dad said, was to trust in God. To know you had a place in heaven. That you didn't have to be afraid of the mysteries of his universe.

Or think that you should be able to solve them all.

CHAPTER 22

After I finished writing in my journal, I found Dad in the quiet common area of our mini-dome.

I rolled my wheelchair up to where he sat, drinking coffee and staring at nothing in the darkness.

"You couldn't sleep either, huh?"

"No," I answered.

We sat together for a while, neither of us speaking.

I had too many thoughts in my head. I didn't know where to begin.

"I wish I didn't have to go," he said. "I'm going to miss you."

In a few days he'd be leaving again, on another shuttle run to Earth. And taking Dr. Jordan with him. Now that Rawling knew Dr. Jordan had been sent here for a weapons test, he'd ordered him deported to Earth.

"I'm going to miss you, Dad. A lot."

More silence.

He put his hand on my shoulder.

"Dad, in my thoughts, I keep hearing some of the last things Ashley ever said to me."

Dad waited.

I heard her words clearly up on the telescope platform, the night before the Hammerhead's test mission: *Tyce, I can't tell you. It would hurt too many others. Even that is saying too much.*

"There was a lot about her we didn't know," I said to Dad.

He let me continue.

Ashley's words rang in my head: *Tyce, please. Help me. Telling you what I know could cost me my life.*

I had not helped her. I had not trusted her. And that made me incredibly sad. I owed her more than that, even if she wasn't here. And it had taken her life to make me want to help.

Remember I told you I grew up in Denver. I didn't. That's the lie I'm supposed to tell everyone.

"Would you help me, Dad?"

"Yes," he said. "With what?"

In the darkness, I blinked back tears. Dad hadn't asked me first with what. He'd simply said *yes.* He trusted me.

There are others. Like us. And we are their only hope.

"I want to find out about Ashley. Where she came from. Who she really is. When you get back to Earth, can you do what you can and send E-mails?"

Dad squeezed my shoulder. "I'll do everything I can. You have my promise."

"Thanks, Dad."

There are others. Like us. And we are their only hope.

I didn't know who "they" were. Or where they were. Or what they needed to give them hope. But Ashley was now gone.

That left me.

EPILOGUE

I didn't sleep well that night.

Dreams I couldn't remember kept waking me up.

I sat up once, calling Ashley's name into the darkness. Then it came back to me what she'd done. And I cried into my pillow for a long time.

In the morning, I didn't want to get out of bed. Getting dressed and getting into my wheelchair would mean that the day had started. And when the day started, I'd have to admit to myself that Ashley was gone.

Except, when I finally pulled myself into sitting position, something shiny caught my eye on the seat of my wheelchair.

It was tiny and silver.

In the shape of a cross.

An earring.

Like the one on a silver chain around my neck.

I felt for mine, wondering if it had somehow fallen off.

It hadn't. It was still there.

With the matching one on the seat of my wheelchair.

As if someone had placed it there while I slept.

Ashley?

WHY DO BAD THINGS HAPPEN?

Have you ever wondered why bad things happen? Why your little sister had to go into the hospital? Why your grandfather died? Why you broke your arm when you fell from the tree? Why the bully at school always seems to get away with picking on your friend?

Throughout this book, Tyce has been asking that question too. Why *does* God allow bad things to happen to people he says he loves? This question is one of the most difficult questions that every person asks sometime in his or her life.

And what you believe about the answer is really important. Why? Because if you decide that God allows bad things to happen because he's weak and can't stop it or because he really doesn't care about us after all, then you won't really want to believe in God. You'll come to think that he doesn't exist after all—except as a character in Bible stories.

Part of why evil exists is because God allows all of us the freedom to make choices—to do good things or bad things. When you choose to do good things, the Earth is a much better place. When you choose to do bad things, you hurt others—and yourself in the long run.

Other people are also making good and bad choices. That's why you'll hear all sorts of bad things happening in the news. (There are lots of good things happening, too, but those events hardly ever make the news.)

But do bad things or the news of bad things mean that God doesn't care?

Since the beginning of the history of writing, hundreds of books have tried to answer this difficult question. Perhaps the best and most famous book on the subject is found in the Bible—the book of Job.

Job loved God, and he was also rich. Then one day, through no fault of his own, he lost his possessions, his children, and his health. No wonder he, too, asked why God allowed suffering.

His friends mistakenly told Job it was because of things he'd done wrong. But Job, through asking questions, learned important things.

He learned that, while suffering might be a consequence of wrong choices, bad things do happen to good people, just as sometimes good things happen to bad people. You can't always control what happens to you, but you can control how you choose to deal with that happening.

Job learned that God was always close to him, even when God might seem far away. This matters a great deal, because we need to believe in God for *who he is,* not what we want him to be. Some people think of God as a Santa or a genie who gives them what they want. But God is really the awesome Creator of the universe who sees the beginning and end of all things. He isn't limited by seeing only this time. And that's why God won't always explain everything to us. There are mysteries we'll never understand while we're on this Earth.

What's the greatest thing Job learned? That even when everything is taken away, he could still trust God. Why? Because God is all we have and need. That truth is both sad and hopeful. It's sad, because someday death will take each of us away from our possessions and our health and our loved ones. But sad as death is, we have an incredible hope. We know that life on Earth, with all its pain, is not our final destination.

No matter what happens around you, you can trust God. Nothing can separate you from his love.

ABOUT THE AUTHOR

Sigmund Brouwer, his wife, recording artist Cindy Morgan, and their daughter split living between Red Deer, Alberta, Canada, and Nashville, Tennessee. He has written several series of juvenile fiction and eight novels. Sigmund loves sports and plays golf and hockey. He also enjoys visiting schools to talk about books. He welcomes visitors to his Web site at www.coolreading.com, where he and a bunch of other authors like to hang out in cyberspace.

MARS DIARIES

DIARIES

are you ready?

Set in an experimental community on Mars in the years 2039–2043, the Mars Diaries feature teen virtual-reality specialist Tyce Sanders. Life on the red planet is not always easy, but it is definitely exciting. As Tyce explores his strange surroundings, he also finds that the mysteries of the planet point to his greatest discovery—a new relationship with God.

MISSION 1: OXYGEN LEVEL ZERO
Time was running out...

MISSION 2: ALIEN PURSUIT
"Help me!" And the radio went dead....

MISSION 3: TIME BOMB
A quake rocks the red planet, uncovering a long kept secret....

MISSION 4: HAMMERHEAD
I was dead center in the laser target controls....

MISSION 5: SOLE SURVIVOR
Scientists buried alive at cave-in site!

MISSION 6: MOON RACER
Everyone has a motive...and secrets. The truth must be found before it's too late.

MISSION 7: COUNTDOWN
20 soldiers, 20 neuron rifles. There was nowhere to run. Nowhere to hide...

MISSION 8: ROBOT WAR
Ashley and I are their only hope, and they think we're traitors.

MISSION 9: MANCHURIAN SECTOR
I was in trouble...and I couldn't trust anyone.

MISSION 10: LAST STAND
Invasion was imminent ... and we'd lost all contact with Earth.

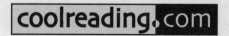